SEPARATE ROOMS

'HE'LL hurt you in the end,' Anya's mother told her. 'He's married; no good can come of it.'

Anya listened to the words of her dying mother but she could not believe them. She was in love with Guy, and when she discovered that he was in love with her she felt there could be no going back.

But she was wrong. She had reckoned without the other woman in the case, and it looked as though both Anya and Guy must accept second best.

This story of a seemingly hopeless love is told with all the emotional impact that her many readers expect from Sonia Deane.

Separate Rooms

❧❧❧

SONIA DEANE

THE ROMANCE BOOK CLUB
121 CHARING CROSS ROAD
LONDON W.C.2

First published 1959

*Printed in Great Britain
by The Anchor Press, Ltd.,
Tiptree, Essex.*

1

ANYA RUTHERFORD plumped up the pillows at her mother's back and felt far more a prisoner than the invalid lying in her cardiac bed. The room was darkening in the gloom of a wet March day, the windows were misted and rain lashed them as the gale heightened.

'You're not going out tonight,' her mother stated aggressively.

'I am.' Anya drew the curtains and switched on a subdued light which threw amber shadows over the moss green carpet and pink quilted hangings.

'To see Guy Latimer, I suppose.'

'Yes,' replied Anya firmly.

'He's married; no good can come of it.' The emaciated figure shuffled a little in her very firm bed. Looking at her mother Anya was reminded of an effigy cut out of faded parchment—mask-like, grotesque. Only the dark beady eyes were alive in that curiously expressionless face, but they had the effect of gimlets piercing Anya's in accusation, condemnation and disgust. 'I should have given you credit for more pride.'

'He doesn't live with his wife,' Anya snapped, her nerves taut, rebellion surging over her.

'Huh! Only because his wife's in Canada. Let her come back and see what would happen.'

'Are you ready for your dinner?' Anya asked coolly.

'No. It's not seven.'

'It's four minutes to seven.'

'That's not seven. . . . And your father's late.'

'I heard the car just now.' Anya sighed. It all seemed so endless, so futile. It was like trying to reach life through a stale, cobweb-filled house.

'Always late. *Business*.' There was suspicion and a cynical dissatisfaction in the utterance, but Anya saw the pain that momentarily clouded her mother's eyes and an instant compassion drove out resentment.

'Lawyers cannot always leave their office exactly to time, Mummie.'

'They can sometimes. . . . But I suppose there isn't very much to come home to.'

'Of course there is. . . .'

'An invalid wife—stuck in this bed like a useless log. The arthritis was bad enough, but now that my heart's bad . . .' It was what she left unsaid that, to Anya, was poignant.

'Daddy doesn't think like that,' she hastened. 'You know how good he is, how concerned for you.'

'Oh, yes. He keeps up that pretence well enough. He must pose as the devoted husband doing *everything* for me; he must play the martyr by seeming not to play it at all, and carry his burden so courageously.' Her eyes wandered around the comfortable room, flower-filled. 'It was always the same; my being ill these past three years hasn't changed anything. I'm like the wife given a mink coat when she aches for one word of affection.' She stopped, shocked by the admission.

Anya moved to the side of the bed and patted her mother's thin, crippled hand. It was one of those rare moments when they were close, and Anya could not honestly contradict a word that had been said.

Harriet Rutherford looked at her with dark intensity and a sudden appeal. 'Make certain the man you marry really loves you, Anya. Don't just go by words because you want to believe them.' Her breathing grew more rapid, her agitation pitiful. 'Guy Latimer,' she gasped, 'he'll hurt you in the end. . . . Listen . . . you must . . . listen . . .' Her voice died

6

away as she made a frightening convulsive movement, and then lay still.

Anya called out in alarm; a call which brought her father to the room. Together they looked down knowing there was nothing that could be done. Harriet Rutherford was dead.

It seemed as though everything after that was confusion. ... No reality touched Anya during the days that followed. She had nursed her mother for three years and felt curiously bereft, without any heartfelt grief. She reacted to necessity with an almost trance-like automation. There was her younger sister, Daphne, to console, although Daphne was incapable of any deep feeling, except for herself, and was her father's favourite—a fact which is no way upset or disturbed Anya, but which she recognized and accepted with the same detachment that she had accepted her life in general. Relatives came and vanished rather like ghosts rousing themselves and then disintegrating.

The Rutherford family was a tradition in Hereford and three generations had followed the legal profession and built up a fine reputation. Rutherford and Son stood for integrity and it was natural—and necessary—for Marcus to maintain that same integrity in his home life—even if as a façade. His house, Wyvern Close, was discreetly concealed from prying eyes and its size—not too large or too small— maintained this discretion. Marcus was proud of his success and he had turned his wife's illness into an asset, knowing that his attitude towards it was approved and admired, not only by his intimate circle of friends, but by his acquaintances, the term, 'Such a devoted husband; adores his wife and children,' being the label he most cherished. But in the cherishing was the cold objective mind of the man, seeing only the aggrandizement it brought to him, rather than being involved and identified with it in genuine appreciation or sincerity. He felt as he walked through the streets of the old-world cathedral city that he was a figure in its daily life. He liked that. Harriet's illness had, in fact, become an asset and

7

since he had loved her only in the first flush of an early marriage—and long since ceased to desire her either as a woman or as a companion—her incapacity had caused him no discomfort. And since Anya had been prepared to take over the nursing responsibilities—thus emphasizing anew the closely knit ties of the family—the financial aspect had not been crippling.

Anya ran the house with the aid of a daily help and a 'treasure' who was always ready to come in, cook a meal and wash it up. On the whole, Harriet's condition had given him freedom since any harmless pleasure he might wish to indulge was grudged him by none. He had never had the courage to take a mistress, and because inwardly he regretted this cowardice he condemned vigorously anyone whose morals would not bear close inspection. He could not deceive even himself that his religious scruples were involved as a prevention of infidelity.

Now, the funeral over, the house restored to normality, he looked at Anya with anxious speculation. He didn't understand her, but told himself that he was not expected to do so. Everyone around him, whether in business or in the home, was a cog in a large wheel which revolved only at his touch and it was sufficient that his children obeyed him for no better reason than that he insisted they should. The words, 'because I tell you to do so,' were his theme.

Anya, he thought, was a strange girl. Her beauty was undeniable; her face oval, full of expression, her skin a warm shade of brown which made it seem she had retained the first coat of summer tan. Her grey eyes were her dominant feature reflecting every mood. Beside her Daphne, he knew, was far less vital—the honey blonde who could cajole and pout and wheedle her way around him, while always leaving him with the feeling that her professed affection was tinged with insincerity. But Daphne could do no wrong, possibly because his love for her was an emotional outlet, a defence.

Anya sat back in her chair, watching the scene like a

8

spectator at a play. It was, she reflected, a pleasant room and on that Saturday afternoon, sun-rifted; a sun suddenly warm which had brought the first almond trees into bud and, in some cases, into blossom. Around her were familiar things with which she had grown up. A serpentine table, a Sheraton writing desk, tall, elegant, silver candlesticks standing on either side of a Regency mirror. . . . The garden stretched lazily to the banks of the river Wye; in the distance the cathedral tower—beautiful and massive and of red sandstone—could be glimpsed to lend solidity and dignity to the scene.

Daphne, clad in grey jeans and a black jumper, slouched in her chair, petulant and intolerant of the restrictions which death had imposed.

'I think,' began Marcus, 'that we ought to discuss the future.' It was a pronouncement.

Daphne flashed him a beguiling smile. 'What have you in mind, Daddy?'

He looked at Anya. 'I appreciate all you did for your mother,' he said abruptly. 'No one could have looked after her—and us, for that matter—half as well.'

'That's true,' Daphne agreed. 'Anya's the self-sacrificing sort. I suppose I ought to be, but I'm not.'

'There is no reason why you should be,' Marcus hastened. 'The point is that now, Anya, you will be able to have a little more freedom . . . it's all been sad—very sad—but we still'—he coughed discreetly—'have each other. I'd like to think we could continue as we always have done. A united family.'

Anya's heart quickened its beat. She knew that she had either to fight for her independence at that moment, or surrender to her father's subtle domination for the rest of her life.

'I shall value the freedom,' she said with a quiet decisiveness.

Daphne, sensitive to Anya's mood, sat upright in her

chair. Marcus coughed again—a maddening habit—and muttered, 'Of course, of course.'

'Yes,' Anya went on, 'I'm going to take a job. Now that Mother is dead I intend to begin to live.'

Her words had an almost electric effect. Daphne cried fearfully: 'You mean that—that you're leaving here or—or something?'

Marcus rapped out: 'Of course Anya doesn't mean that. The matter of taking a job can be discussed. I'm sure that leaving home doesn't come into it.'

Anya's voice was steady. 'I'm afraid it does, Daddy. I want to get away.'

Marcus saw his orderly life, his well-run house, his creature comforts vanishing. 'That is quite impossible,' he said absurdly. 'We need you here and——'

'You have Daphne,' Anya reminded him coolly. 'Because she never has accepted any responsibility it doesn't mean that she never will. I'm twenty-four and have a perfect right to make my own decisions.'

Daphne glowered, her face petulant and angry.

'If,' she shouted, 'you think I'm going to be an unpaid housekeeper you're very much mistaken.' She stopped because of the expression on Anya's face.

Anya smiled—a wry, faintly cynical smile. 'Thank you for summing up my position so neatly.'

Marcus was out of his depth. He didn't know whether to attack, or to appeal to what he knew to be Anya's warm, generous nature. He chose the former. 'You don't deceive me,' he said with a merciless biting accusation. 'Guy Latimer's at the bottom of this. It isn't because you want to take a job, or really to leave home, but because you want to get away somewhere where you can pursue your—your . . .' He spluttered.

'My—what?' Anya had never felt so calm. No emotion stirred within her, only determination.

'Your relationship with him. But I warn you'—his face

10

reddened in anger—'if you bring disrepute upon this family you'll——'

Daphne said wearily: 'Oh, for heaven's sake don't start behaving like the heavy father in some melodrama. I couldn't care less what Anya does, so long as she's here.'

Anya's hands clenched. 'I have no relationship as you call it with Guy—other than friendship. But if I had, your attitude wouldn't exactly sway me to your point of view.'

'And just what job do you think you're capable of getting? Marcus gained a little confidence.

'A hotel receptionist's job,' Anya told him calmly.

At that he laughed. 'With what qualifications?'

'Typing, shorthand, French and German,' she flashed back at him. 'Hotel staff problems are no less acute than those of ordinary houses. If I can, I'd like to begin at a smallish place—like The Speech House—and see what comes along afterwards.'

'And the fact that Guy lives in Coleford, a matter of a few miles away from there, has no bearing on such a choice,' Marcus exclaimed.

'I wouldn't say that,' came the honest reply. 'Anyway I'm in touch with the hotel.'

Marcus got up from his chair, lit a cigarette, flung away the match with a fierce and angry gesture. 'I just can't believe it.'

Anya stared at him. 'Did you seriously imagine I could go on living as I have done for the past four years—that is after Mummie was dead? I'm not the heroine in some early Victorian novel. I don't regret anything I did in the way of nursing, but I've no intention of letting life slip away now, believe me.'

'But what about the house . . . me? Your sister?'

'The house will need a housekeeper unless Daphne is ready to take over where I leave off. You will have to revise your life in any case—and probably—later on—marry again.'

11

'How dare you!' Marcus was immediately defensive because the thought had been chasing through his mind, quickening his pulse, even as Anya had been talking.

'Oh, Daddy,' Anya said impatiently, 'can't you come down off that holier-than-thou pedestal for a second, and talk like a human being? Or is that you so love being the martyr that you'd deprive yourself even of happiness in order to perpetuate the idea.'

Daphne said penetratingly: 'The broken-hearted widower has much to recommend it.' She looked at her father and saw him wince. 'Sorry.'

Anya said quietly: 'We've lived with pretence long enough. Now the reason for the pretence has gone . . . the façade is no longer necessary, and you've nothing to put in its place. I intend to find something.'

Daphne lolled back in her chair again. 'Anya's right, of course. . . . How about tea. I'm famished.'

Marcus said sharply: 'I should have thought you could have contributed something a little more helpful to this—this discussion.'

'Sorry, Daddy. . . . Not to worry. All be the same in a thousand years. Why get in a flap? I still want my tea.'

Anya got up from her chair. She said without malice, but with the calm of a person commenting upon the weather: 'I should get it if I were you, Daphne. I shan't be in. In fact I shan't be home until late tonight.'

Daphne gasped. 'But what about dinner?'

'I suggest you cook it for a change. There's plenty of food in the house.'

'I shall do no such thing.'

'Then you'll get very hungry, won't you?'

Marcus stared at Anya as though she had suddenly become a stranger whose presence was fantastic.

'I wouldn't have thought it possible you'd behave like this.'

Anya sighed. 'Listen, Daddy, if I'd tried to discuss my

own problems with you, ease you gently into this situation, you'd have been as obstructive and destructive as you possibly could, and we'd have ended up without any settlement—only frayed tempers. You've lived so long outside my world that it has become foreign to you. Statements, therefore, are the kindest things for us all.'

'But,' he gasped, out of his depth, 'you've always taken the reins, I mean——' Again his face reddened.

'I've always accepted my responsibilities because of Mummie's illness,' she said quietly. 'You and Daphne have benefited. I did my job. Now I'm giving it up. It is really very simple. I'm handing the reins over to Daphne who has never, to my knowledge, done a thing for anyone in her life. It will be excellent training for her to start now.'

Daphne had shot out of her chair. 'That's what you think,' she shouted. 'I loathe house work; I detest cooking. . . . Anya, listen . . .'

But Anya had gone.

Upstairs in her bedroom she sat down on her dressing-table stool and looked at herself in the Regency mirror. Excitement brightened her eyes. Death had not only released her mother, it had also released her and it would be hypocritical to deny the fact. Her conscience had been far stronger than her affection during those years of nursing, but she had the satisfaction that she had done all she possibly could, and had thus earned her freedom.

.   .   .   .   .   .

Guy Latimer awaited her at their appointed meeting place on the banks of the river Wye, where the shimmering trees dipped the shadow of their lacy outline in the still, sunlit waters and across its indigo ribbon, the cathedral spire loomed graceful and yet solid against a cloudless blue sky.

'Anya.'

Their eyes met in wordless appeal. She thought how strong and tanned he looked; how the fine lines running away from his eyes suggested a man accustomed to the sun. Not good-looking, but with a charm that drew people to him. She didn't try to deceive herself about her feelings for him. She had been in love with him for many months and their casual meetings, their friendship, had brought a great hunger, never quite so great, or so unendurable, as now. It wasn't easy to gauge his feelings, for he was not an effusive man given to pretty speeches, and at times, after leaving him, she had felt so bleak and empty that she had vowed never to meet him again, only to find herself listening in an agony of suspense for the sound of his voice on the telephone; and when she heard it her resolution would fade to a desperate need of him. Her mother's words came back. 'Guy Latimer. . . . He'll hurt you in the end.' A shiver went over her and defiance counteracted fear. She said lamely: 'It's been quite a time . . . I mean——' She broke off, confused. Guy had attended the funeral, but she had spoken only a few words to him.

'A month,' he answered quietly. 'I was sorry about your mother. . . . It will make a very great difference to you.'

They sat down on a nearby seat. The day was still, as though the world were relaxing in its afternoon siesta. Everything seemed suddenly unreal to Anya because she couldn't fully grasp the fact that the door of her cage had opened.

'Yes.' She looked at him contemplatively, trying to fight against a surging emotion. 'I'm going to take a job. I've already told my father.'

'What sort of a job?'

Guy Latimer was trying to find the courage to tell her how he felt. What had seemed an easy task now became an ordeal because he was desperately afraid of being misunderstood. As she sat there, the sunlight falling upon her face, it was almost as though she were suddenly remote from him, living in a different world. Their friendship, he knew, had been unusual; their brief meetings without apparent emotion of any kind, yet the mere fact of those meetings establishing an irrevocable truth.

'Hotel—receptionist, or something of that kind, until I get used to things.' She gave a little nervous laugh. 'I suppose I'll have to learn to live.'

'You want to leave Hereford?'

'No, but I'll have to go where the job is.'

He sighed.

'I'd hoped,' she went on, 'for The Speech House, but I was too late. I telephoned them before I came out. They'd already engaged someone.'

'That would have been ideal—so near Coleford,' Guy hastened. The implication was obvious. He owned Green Meadows, a seven-hundred-and-fifty-acre farm near there, and on the edge of the Forest of Dean in which The Speech House was situated.

Anya nodded. 'I suppose I shall have to try London.' She was watching his face for any change of expression, held by a suspense fast becoming a torment. What *did* he feel about her? *That would have been ideal!* Was she mad to assume the words meant that he wanted to keep her near him or, alternatively, was he thinking that she would be within reasonable distance of her father's house?

He twisted around on the seat, his arm sliding along its back so that his hand almost touched her shoulder.

'Don't go away, Anya,' he said tensely.

Hope touched her, bringing the colour to her cheeks as she whispered: 'I don't want to go, Guy, but——'

'I love you.' His eyes met hers in passionate fervour. 'I've ached to tell you, but I've had nothing to offer.'

'You call love nothing?' Happiness trembled in her voice. 'Oh, Guy,' she added shakenly.

His hands gripped her shoulders. 'You mean—you——'

'I love you too,' she whispered.

15

'I'm married, Anya. It could mean hell, heartbreak and I've no earthly right,' he said fiercely, 'to have told you.'

'If you knew how awful it has been—wondering. The misery and the emptiness.'

'I fought against you, heaven knows.' His hands dropped from her shoulders.

For Anya just then the knowledge of his love was enough. It filled her heart with a happiness she had never before known, or dreamed of knowing. There was no past, no future, only that enchanted world where dreams made mock of reality. *Guy loved her.* . . . *Loved her.* . . . She looked at him almost shyly and he took her hands in his, holding them for a brief second and then letting them go as passers-by approached.

'Listen, darling,' he began urgently, 'I'm going to do all I can to get a divorce. Those words can sound so glib, but Monica left me and, as you know, went to Canada two and a half years ago. In six months I can get my freedom on the grounds of desertion. I intended waiting before I told you how I felt—waiting until the three years were up.' He made a little gesture of appeal. 'Seeing you today, realizing that your mother's death . . .' He tried to think of the right words, but emotion tore at him. 'You *know* . . . don't you?'

'Yes. I've been tied too—in a vastly different way.' Pain clouded her eyes. 'How could I have left Mummie? She had so little.'

'I can understand that.'

'But without your friendship'—she paused and her gaze rested in his—'I don't think I could have gone on. You'll never know what seeing you, talking to you, has meant to me.'

'Darling . . .' he said abruptly, 'what time have you to be back?'

She relaxed as though some unseen hand had smoothed away tension and anxiety. 'My own time.'

'Let's drive to the farm—I want to talk to you, to be

16

alone with you. I can't kiss you here with people wandering around,' he added in frustration.

'I'd like to go to Green Meadows more than anywhere,' Her smile was adoring as well as provocative. 'And I'd rather like to be kissed.'

They drove back through the unspoiled countryside of Herefordshire, into Gloucestershire with its deep valleys, its forests, its haunting old-world appeal, until they came to the farm on the outskirts of the Forest of Dean. Originally it had been a manor house, returned to Guy's family at the time of the Restoration and from then handed down and, finally, when Guy's great-grandfather inherited it, adapted— for financial reasons—into an agricultural project from which had emerged the farm of today.

Anya gazed at it, her heart filled with yearning. To live there, to be Guy's wife . . . She looked at him as the car stopped outside the corinthian pillared, white house—two storeyed—and said breathlessly: 'There's an atmosphere here . . . I can't explain.'

He said with swift appreciation: 'I know. . . . One either loves all its stands for, or one does not.' His expression was grim as he added: 'Monica loathed living here.'

Anya wanted to know about Monica. She had never met or seen her; she knew only what she had heard of Mrs Latimer and gossip had not been kind.

'I suppose we all have different ideas and cannot be blamed for them.

'True.' He helped her from the car. 'But we do not need to pretend that we like a thing simply to gain a material advantage.'

Anya tensed. Was that the answer to the failure of the marriage?

They went inside the square cool hall, with its wide stone fireplace, its hunting trophies and gleaming copper. Graves who—with his wife—looked after the place, came forward inquiringly.

'It's all right, Graves,' Guy hastened. 'I wasn't expected back, I know. . . . But do you think your wife could manage a cold supper for two? In about an hour?'

Anya smiled at Graves whom she had seen on a previous visit.

'Indeed, sir.'

'Any calls?'

'One, sir. The lady would not give her name.'

Guy shot him an inquiring look. 'Obviously not a voice you recognized.'

'No, sir.'

Anya struggled to ignore what seemed to be Guy's sudden uneasiness.

'Probably,' he explained, 'my sister. She's been in South America for the past three years and always tries to be mysterious when she gets back.'

'She said she would ring again, sir.'

'That could mean tomorrow or in another three years.'

Anya exclaimed breathlessly: 'But surely she would have let you know of her return . . . I mean——' She broke off awkwardly.

'You don't know Norah,' he grinned.

They went into what had once been the drawing-room and was now a comfortable living-room, book lined, flower filled, its long windows looking out over the green farm lands which tilted against the evening sky like a giant painting. For a second they stood, eyes meeting, emotion surging passionately and inescapably as his arms went around her with a suffocating closeness, and his lips met hers as she clung to him in a wild, breathless ecstasy as though she would defy any fate ever to part them. Her hands reached up to his neck, drawing him nearer in all the rapture which, until then, had been part of a dream into which had gone all the hunger and yearning of desire.

'Oh, Guy,' she whispered as she drew back and then rested weakly against him. 'I love you so *much*.'

18

He looked down at her rather like a man disbelieving his own happiness, his good fortune. 'I must never hurt you,' he said roughly, his hand pressing her head against his shoulder in a gentle protecting gesture.

'*He'll hurt you in the end.*'

Anya's body suddenly sagged and became a weight against his. An empty, desolate sensation stole upon her as she asked: 'Why do you say that?' Her eyes as they met his were dark and appealing, almost frightened.

'*Darling.*' There was a note of shocked surprise in his voice. 'What is it?'

She sighed and recovered. 'Stupidity,' she managed to answer. 'The feeling that this can't be quite real—my being here and your loving me.'

'It is real,' he said quietly.

Her eyes shone again, starry and adoring as she looked at him. 'You could never hurt me except by pretence.' She held his gaze.

'Pretence?'

'About your feelings.'

'Then I shall never hurt you,' he promised. 'I love you—deeply, Anya. Always remember that.' His words were measured and seemed like a dedication. 'Will you,' he added solemnly, 'marry me when I'm free, my darling?'

Happiness surged back, all sufficing, sending her into his arms again. 'Yes, oh, yes,' she answered tremulously.

Gaiety touched the edge of passion as he said: 'Champagne! That's what we need, darling. This is one of those moments we can never live again—only remember.' Still keeping his arm about her, he moved to the bell switch and when Graves appeared, said, trying to sound casual: 'Graves, put that bottle of Pol Roger, 1947, on ice, will you?'

'Certainly, sir.' Graves' expression was inscrutable. The door closed behind him.

Guy laughed. 'I don't think I've ever drunk champagne in this house since he's been with me.'

19

Anya asked: 'How long has he been here?'

'Just about two and a half years—immediately after Monica left.'

Monica. . . . His wife. . . .

It struck Anya then how very little she knew about that marriage and how rarely he had spoken of personal things. Their friendship, while deep, had flourished at a level which made questioning unnecessary. It was enough, she had told herself, just to be with him, to listen to his voice and to pray that one day he might love her. . . . Suddenly, almost sharply, that phase had gone; suddenly even the room in which she sat was haunted by a woman she had never seen, yet whose life completely dominated their future.

'Tell me about Monica,' she said quietly. 'I've never asked.'

'And I was reluctant to talk of the past until I could see some light for the future.'

'You'd been married four years, hadn't you, when she left?'

'Yes.' He lit a cigarette and as Anya sat down he stood before her and then perched himself on the arm of her chair. 'Four wretched years,' he added tensely. 'Perhaps we were both too young; too immature emotionally. She'd had an unhappy life—a broken home and all that went with it.'

'Was she—attractive?' Anya felt that an invisible hand was squeezing her heart.

'Yes—the rather appealing, helpless type. Fair, doll-like. We met at a dance and we believed it was love at first sight.' His gaze rested inquiringly upon Anya. 'Have you ever loved before this, Anya?'

'I thought I had. . . .'

'Graham Collins?'

'Yes,' she answered amazed, 'how did you know?'

'Guesswork, darling. He's still in love with you, isn't he?'

'I'm afraid so.'

Guy said almost bitterly: 'He's a free man, your father's

20

junior partner—a clever lawyer. Everything to recommend him.'

'Not if I am in love with you.'

He picked up her hand and trailed her fingers across his mouth. 'Are you *sure*?'

'Very sure.'

'And where does Graham fit into the picture?'

'As a friend. I never at any time promised to marry him. He was just someone always there. It wasn't until he asked me to be his wife that I knew how adolescent my feelings for him really were. An excitement, if you like, associated with first love. Then when mother became so ill, marriage, in any case, seemed an impossibility.'

'I could be thankful for your mother's need of you,' Guy said quietly.

Anya leaned forward, resting against his shoulder. 'Why did Monica go away?'

He didn't hesitate. 'She inherited a considerable amount of money which made her independent.'

Anya raised a startled gaze to his. 'You mean——'

'I mean that money enabled her to see behind the façade of our marriage. Shall we say that I served a purpose. . . . I'm not blaming her, quite possibly she didn't realize just how much the advantages of financial security were bound up with marriage to me.'

'How did you feel when she—she left?' Anya tried to make her voice sound normal, but every nerve in her body seemed to ache with a curious fear and uncertainty.

'A mixture of everything,' he admitted honestly. 'Even though sub-consciously I'd known our marriage to be a mistake, I hated having to face the truth of it.' He looked at Anya pleadingly, almost appealingly. 'I want to give you as realistic a picture as I can. I suppose we all hate failure. It touches our pride and I'd thought in terms of permanency, of children——'

'I see,' Anya murmured, feeling sick with jealousy.

He shot her a quick, perceptive glance. 'But I was not even then *in love* with her, darling.' As he spoke he drew Anya close holding her tightly, almost possessively. 'The point is that if every marriage broke up for that reason alone, how many would survive?'

'Meaning that, for your part, you would never have left her?'

He hesitated. 'Can I answer that honestly? I didn't know you then. But if you ask me if *at that time* I should have broken up my marriage because I realized that I was no longer in love with my wife, then I must say no.'

Anya nodded. 'I think I understand.'

'I want you to, darling. I can't wholly condemn Monica for leaving me, make her action an excuse, when I know in my heart that her going wasn't a tragedy so far as I was concerned. A shock, yes. It's so difficult to explain emotion. All I can tell you is that I never—*never* loved her as I love you. This is complete, mature. . . . If you could only know how much you've meant to me; how I've longed to tell you how I felt and to be free.' His gaze was troubled. 'Now you see what I mean by hurting you.'

She put her cheek against his. 'You won't hurt me. . . . Thank you for being so honest—so fair.' Her gaze met his. 'I shall tell my father the truth,' she added resolutely.

Guy's voice was low and yet authoritative as he answered: 'That is one thing I must ask you not to do.'

2

GUY watched the dismay and consternation that flashed instantly into Anya's eyes and hastened: 'Darling, please don't misunderstand me. It certainly isn't through any desire for secrecy, but because until I'm free, I must be careful. I've already gone into all this with my solicitor. Heaven knows I don't want to prejudice my case. Not only that, I want to *be* free and tell him the facts myself. Now, from his point of view, I should be suspect.'

'I can appreciate that,' Anya said with relief.

Guy held her gaze very steadily. 'We could become lovers, my darling, and I could ask the discretion of the court—that is the only alternative to our remaining friends and meeting occasionally. The imbecility of the divorce laws is beyond belief.'

Anya's head lifted slightly, her body was taut as though expressing the defiance within her. 'Would you like us to become lovers?'

Emotion seemed alive in the sudden silence.

'Not nearly so much as I would like to become your husband,' he answered sincerely.

Tenderness welled within her. 'Thank you,' she whispered.

'If we were lovers,' he went on quietly, 'I could not conceal the fact and one never knows just how much it might weaken my case. Fighting from strength is always a good thing—and that applies to anything your father may have to say, also.'

'Nothing he says could ever influence me.'

'That may be so, darling, but I'd prefer not to cause any

23

unpleasantness. Oh, Anya, we've a lifetime ahead of us—so much to do, to see. So much happiness. I don't want the shadows for you and I want your trust—that above all.'

She got up and gave him both her hands and there was a sudden peace within her as she said: 'You have it, Guy—utterly. I know you're right. Already Daddy is suspicious of our friendship and the truth might be a weapon in his hands.'

'I want my freedom,' Guy said, and there was a fierce determination in his eyes. 'As things are the divorce will not involve anything more than a technicality. The facts speak for themselves. The waiting will be an ordeal, naturally, but if we understand each other . . . Darling——' He broke off abruptly and then said: 'Now how about that champagne?'

They went into the dining-room where a cold meal awaited them. Graves hovered and Guy said with a smile: 'All right, Graves. I'll ring if I need you.'

Anya looked at the retreating figure. 'Good man?'

'Very. He and Martha run the place well. No bother. She's a tartar on occasion and they have their fights, but they're a happy couple really. My mother'—he paused—'she will like you, Anya—Mother thinks they're far too free and easy, but Mother is a bit of a stickler. Still lives in pre-war days, thinks modern life atrocious, won't have a television set and regards picnic meals as barbaric! My father accepts her pattern for living because it suits him. He does a spot of writing for agricultural papers. Crippled with arthritis, but manages to get by with the aid of a tape recorder. His study is his world.'

'They live on the farm, I believe?'

'Yes. Father built a small house when he retired from farming.' Guy turned as he spoke and indicated a spot far out on a distant hill top where it was possible to distinguish a white blob. 'There. It looks over the valley to the Wye and at the back of it you can see Symonds Yat. Mother loves her garden and runs the place with daily help.'

24

Anya gazed at the splendour of the view. Green Meadows stood on a plateau looking down and across the Wye valley with its deeply wooded slopes, its vivid greens and soft purples, its serene river tinted crimson by the reflection of the setting sun. It seemed that here was eternity.

'It's so utterly beautiful,' she said in awe.

Guy moved and stood behind her, holding her arms and drawing her shoulders against him.

'Especially by moonlight,' he murmured. 'You will see it then, Anya . . . and in summer and in snow, dearest. You'll make this old house what it has never really been to me—home. I've always loved it, but now, through you, it has come to life.'

She turned to meet his lips and they clung together, breaking away only when emotion seemed almost unbearable.

Guy placed her chair in position, and took his place near her, beginning to carve the chicken.

'My first meal here,' she said, taking in details of the room; the Henry VIII panelling, the two very good paintings, the richly carved sideboard and, lastly, the highly polished oval table at which they sat. Two large silver candlesticks stood on either side of a silver rose bowl filled with deep red roses. 'Martha is quite an artist,' she added, indicating the flowers.

'Her pet hobby—arranging flowers,' Guy said. 'We can keep her on, darling, or change the routine completely later on. It will be entirely up to you.'

It was impossible, Anya thought, to grasp the fact that one day this would be her home; that she would be mistress of it . . .able to make decisions, to plan, to look after Guy as only a woman who deeply loves a man could ever do. His quiet confidence, his attitude suggestive of the inevitability of their future together, filled her with an overwhelming happiness.

'You said that your mother will like me . . . but will she

altogether approve of me, do you think? The two things need not be compatible!'

Guy lifted the champagne from an improvised ice bed.

'Don't boast a bucket,' he grinned. Then: 'Mother's liking a person is about the maximum of what I judge to be her capacity for emotional feeling. She's detached, if you know what I mean. Undemonstrative and absorbed in her own affairs. Not in the least narrow-minded if that is what you wondered.'

'It was.'

The cork shot across the room, the champagne over-flowed the first glass.

A second later they drank, looking at each other, feeling the glow of ecstasy, the thrill of love newly confessed.

'We must make a habit of this,' Guy said softly.

'Invent celebrations as an excuse.'

'A woman's favourite pastime,' he teased.

The shadow of Monica crept stealthily into the room. How often had he drunk champagne with *her*, sitting at that very table? Sickness surged like an illness she could not escape.

Guy put out his hand. 'I have never drunk champagne like this before, darling.'

Colour burned in Anya's cheeks. 'Were my thoughts so noisy?'

'Yes.'

'Oh, dear!'

They laughed together.

'A wife seems so very much more real than nebulous *women*,' Anya admitted.

'I can appreciate that. And there haven't been any nebu-lous women!' He added: 'You've been too much in my thoughts for me even to notice them.'

'When,' she asked, 'did you first know about me?'

'One evening—almost two years ago—when we met by chance outside the cathedral.'

26

'I remember. You were so cold and aloof that I decided you'd no time for me at all!'

He smiled at her indulgently. 'My defence against you, darling.'

They sat very still in the gathering dusk. Words had become unnecessary. The silence was broken when Anya said: 'My idea of getting a job—a hotel job—don't you agree that it is a good one?'

Guy felt a pang of jealousy, a possessiveness. He wanted her with him.

'In the circumstances probably it is. You don't want to stay at home?'

'No. Anything but that. I can like my father, remain friendly with him, if I get away. Not otherwise.'

'I know of a hotel that's just opened—The Old Grange— right on the edge of the forest. It belonged to Sir Nicholas Brent who died last year. A syndicate bought it up when the family put it on the market. I'm very friendly with Jimmy Fawcett who is manager there. I could put you in touch with him.'

'That would be ideal. Not too far away from you and yet not obviously near.'

He nodded agreement. 'I think their plan is to encourage the tourist trade, build up the district and its history.'

'Then if we get masses of French and German guests my languages will help!'

'I know; Jimmy said only the other day that staff problems were his real headache. I have a contract with them for poultry.'

Anya gazed at him with a new interest. 'I never really see you as a farmer. Did you always want to be one?'

'No. I wanted to write plays. After scrapping four, I realized that farming would have to pay for my hobby. And when my father's health worsened . . . I'd no alternative but to carry on. He lost a packet over some dud shares and we're only just beginning to get back on an even

27

keel.' He looked at her very searchingly. 'I'm not a rich, or even a well-to-do, man, Anya. We can live well here because we produce almost everything we need, but I can't afford a world cruise as a honeymoon trip, or to wrap you in mink.'

She puckered her brows. 'Do you imagine that I'm interested in your financial position?'

'No, but on the other hand it is reasonable for a woman to want to know just what she is marrying into—the degree of security, if you like.'

'You were thinking of Monica.'

'Yes. It was a blow to her to discover that I was not a rich farmer. It didn't occur to me to go into all the details of my position with her. She didn't appear to be interested in money—until afterwards.'

'And do you fear lest I might be?'

Instantly his hand closed over hers. 'No, darling; only that I prefer you to know the facts. Green Meadows has, in effect, to keep two homes—my father's and this one.'

'Then I shall not need two people to look after us when I am your wife,' she said with emphasis. 'Daily help will be enough.'

He shook his head. 'Oh, no! That isn't an economy I want to make. You can help far more with the paper work, accounts, so *many* things, Anya. Graves pulls his weight and does an amazing amount in the garden. He isn't just a manservant as might be supposed—a luxury. And Martha attends to all manner of things outside the house. In their way they're unique. That's why I cannot expect—even if I wished for it, which I don't—the place to be run as meticulously as my mother would choose!'

'I know what you mean. You want to relax, not to worry about conventional behaviour!'

'Exactly. . . . Oh, Anya . . .' He paused. 'I love your name quite apart from your association with it.'

28

'It was my great-grandmother's name. I've never been able to understand its Russian flavour. We're solidly British for generations!'

He looked at her with rapt gaze, his mind and heart filled with the joy, the intense and overwhelming happiness, she had brought into his life.

'You want children?' he asked almost abruptly.

'Very much. A family, Guy. I want to give them all the things I've missed—oh, not in the material sense, but the parental. Friendship, understanding—a kind of emotional harbour, if you know what I mean.'

'I know—very well. I feel that, too. I missed it, also.' His hand tightened upon hers in an almost fierce clasp. 'We've so much, darling . . . to be here like this, to talk, to dream, to discuss things. Really to know each other instead of a superficial acceptance of the people we seem to be.'

Later they went over the house together, planning, looking ahead to the day when they would call it theirs, when the waiting was over, the suspense forgotten. There was little in it to be changed, for Anya could not fault what had been Guy's mother's taste in its embellishment. Only Monica's room—unused, rather dreary and according to her taste—provided a subject for discussion.

Guy, looking around it, at its olive greens and rusts, said casually: 'Monica always had her own room. She considered separate rooms civilized.'

Anya looked up at him and a great weight seemed suddenly to be lifted from her heart even though she knew the reaction to be rather absurd since, after all, Monica had been his wife in every sense of the word. But this left her an *intimacy*, something new to be shared with him, something so valuable that a lump rose in her throat in overwhelming gratitude.

'And do you take that view?' she asked breathlessly.

He put his arms around her and looked deeply, earnestly down into her eyes as he said: 'Not now. And now I realize

29

that accepting it before—as I did from the very beginning
—proved how very little I knew about love.'

Anya's arms reached up and encircled his neek, her cheek
pressed against his as they held each other tightly and with a
tenderness that was as great an expression of their love as
passion.

For her it was a moment of sweetness, of utter trust. For
him it was reward and fulfilment.

3

A FEW days later Anya went for an interview with James Fawcett at The Old Grange. It stood looking over the Wye valley, taking in part of the view from Yat rock. Illimitable views encompassed it on all sides and its tall Elizabethan chimneys towered above the tree tops, seeming to become part of the sky.

Anya felt a pang for its lost glory; for days when courtiers and their ladies had walked its smooth lawns, when brocades had rustled and the music of spinets had echoed thinly on the summer breeze. Now, its wide semi-circular drive was lined with cars, and as she went into the impressive hall with its imposing staircase sweeping up to the first floor and then curving away to be lost from sight at the fourth, the impact of modernity was almost shattering. The flunkeys had gone; the cool serenity had given place to an urgent activity and to white-jacketed stewards expertly attending to orders for cocktails.

James Fawcett turned out to be a tall, broad-shouldered man with a faint lilt of the Scottish accent. His eyes were merry and very blue; his mouth good-tempered and his skin a deep tan.

'You're Miss Rutherford,' he said in welcome. 'Guy rang me about you. If half he said was true you're a gift from heaven. How soon can you start?'

She stared at him. 'But you——'

'I know of your father, your background and that you've not had a job before,' he said with a touch of humour. 'That could be an asset if the qualifications of those who

31

know precisely nothing when it comes to it is anything to go by! And you speak French. Wonderful. Can't understand a word of it myself and that doesn't help when you get a number of French people staying here—as we do.'

Anya laughed, relaxed and knew she could work there. 'I could start tomorrow,' she told him.

'Splendid! Mind you, you'll be engaged as a receptionist, but heaven knows what your work will embrace. Depends entirely on who walks out and when. It's the isolation of the place. It appeals to the guests, but damned if the staff are sold on it. With you, having local contacts, it should be different.' He shot her a swift glance. 'Engaged?'

'No,' she said honestly.

'Splendid.'

'But that doesn't mean I've any intention of being an old maid!'

'Naturally and obviously. I'd settled for even a year's peace.'

'I think I could guarantee you that, Mr. Fawcett.'

He beamed at her. Then: 'You've known Guy for long?'

'Two years or so.'

He nodded. 'We were in training together during the last year of the war.' There was a faint pause. 'I was best man at his wedding.'

Anya's heart felt that it was suddenly moved out of position. Guy had not mentioned the fact. She didn't speak, but gave a little nod of understanding.

'And I might tell you I wasn't happy in my work on that occasion,' James Fawcett added. 'You, of course, haven't met Monica.'

'No.'

'Umm. . . . Difficult to describe. Unfathomable. . . . Now, come along and have a look at the place. You've a pleasant bed-sitting-room, and all the comforts. But it isn't any good my deceiving you about the work. It can be pretty trying. Dealing with people unless you love 'em——'

'I do. They interest me.'

'Splendid,' he said again. It was his favourite word.

'I hope you won't be disappointed in me.'

He shot her an encouraging look. 'I shan't be.'

Anya smiled. 'I feel awfully nervous, you know.'

'You won't, once you get the hang of things. Miss Colby, my secretary, will soon show you the ropes. She's plump and middle-aged and good-natured, as well as efficient. We're a happy staff—at least the hard core of the staff is—it's what I call the floating vote that drives us mad. I've all kinds of ideas for improving things, but to have central heating installed would cost a small fortune, and the syndicate who bought the place have to be convinced that everything is vitally necessary before they'll part with their money!'

Anya met Miss Colby a few minutes later. Una Colby took one look at the new receptionist and decided she'd do. Different from the procession of other languid film-star types who had convinced James Fawcett that they wanted work instead of a husband.

'Don't worry,' she said amiably, 'you'll pick it all up very quickly and I'll help. I'm the Jack-of-all-Trades around here.'

Anya warmed to the friendliness. 'I'll try to lessen that activity.'

James Fawcett flashed Una a knowing glance. 'We've struck lucky this time,' he said with enthusiasm. 'And she can come in tomorrow.'

'No!'

Anya laughed. 'You may regret putting welcome on the mat for me!'

Una Colby grunted. 'We shan't.' Her inflection was praise.

Anya walked back, down the long beech-lined drive, to a spot where Guy had arranged to meet her.

'Well?' His eyes met hers eagerly.

'The job is mine. I was received with open arms. I think they've been having some trouble there.'

'That, my darling, is an understatement.'

Anya looked at him and recalled what James Fawcett had told her.

'Mr. Fawcett mentioned that he was best man at your wedding.'

'Yes. Jimmy and I have been through quite a few experiences together.'

'I liked him.'

'Loyal as they make them. I shall be happy to know you're there, darling—until I can look after you.' He helped her into his car as he spoke. 'Now I'm going to run you back to Hereford.'

'To a discreet 'bus stop!'

'And what is a *discreet* 'bus stop?' he teased.

'One where I can easily reach Wyvern without the family seeing you.'

'I hate that.'

'But it is the wisest thing, Guy.'

'I suppose so,' he said reluctantly. 'When it really comes to putting theory into practice I rebel.' His smile was rueful.

They drove through the gently undulating countryside, where the Wye cut its way, here and there bursting into turbulent haste as it rushed over stony rapids. Villages and farmhouses of black and white half-timbered design were a reminder of the England of Yesterday. Guy kept to the by-roads and then linked up with the A49 for the final run into Hereford where he stopped at The Old House, in High Town, survivor of Jacobean Hereford, in which was stored furniture and County treasures.

'I can walk home from here,' she said confidently.

His hand reached out and clasped hers. 'It's been a perfect evening,' he whispered tenderly.

Just then—the last thing she wanted—Graham Collins pulled his car up beside Guy's as she stepped on to the pavement so that there was no escape. He and Guy were acquainted—that and no more. They exchanged polite

34

greetings and Graham said: 'I was just going over to Wyvern Close.' He looked at Anya who felt the colour mounting her cheeks. 'Can I save you a walk?'

Guy felt a new and resented jealousy. Graham could be so assured in his relationship with Anya. He was a free man. Suppose, after all, she should tire of waiting . . . He dismissed the thought as being an insult to her, but his own insecurity whipped up anger. He fell back on a familiar weapon, a chilly aloofness, almost as though his body had frozen and his lips become paralysed. Anya, glancing at him, tried to break down the barrier in a helpless look of appeal.

Graham stood there—watching. He was full of suspicion and of distrust. What were they doing together those two? And why hadn't Guy gone on to Wyvern? It was obvious from the direction in which the car was facing that they had driven into the town and not come from the house.

Anya said unsteadily: 'Thank you, Graham.'

Graham, assured of her company, expanded a little. 'Don't often see you in Hereford, Latimer.'

'I am often in the town.'

'Market days,' Graham suggested.

'Market days particularly,' Guy agreed coldly. He turned to Anya. 'I'm glad to have been able to drive you back. . . . Good luck tomorrow.' And with that and a mumbled, 'Good night,' his car shot forward exceeding the speed limit as it raced through the town.

Anya felt sick because of a sudden emptiness. Guy might suddenly have dropped out of her world. She looked at Graham knowing that her irritation towards him was unfair.

Graham Collins was one of those tall, athletic types, a Cambridge Blue and keen on sports of all kinds. He had everything to recommend him. His father and her own had been life-long friends, and Graham's entry into Marcus Rutherford's firm had been similar to that of a son carrying

35

on a tradition. Marcus had almost taken it for granted that Anya and Graham would marry. It was the right and proper sequence and part of his overall plan.

Graham had shared this view and, even now, believed that Mrs Rutherford's death would assist him to achieve his ambition. All that Anya needed was time to adjust herself to an entirely different life. That achieved and she would soon come to realize that she cared deeply for him after all. His love for her was sincere and uncomplicated and his lawyer's mind refused to be swayed by any emotion which caused him undue suffering. The fact that she had twice refused to marry him, merely strengthened his determination to succeed.

'I certainly ruffled him,' he said with satisfaction.

'Ruffled?' Anya's voice was querulous.

'I didn't realize that you went out with him.' The words came unguardedly. He knew Anya well enough to appreciate that she would detest interference in her affairs.

'Having been on a string for four years I am making the most of my freedom,' she said, her nerves on edge.

'Meaning to mind my own business?'

Instantly she relented. 'No, Graham. Sorry.'

She looked at him, asking just why she couldn't have fallen in love with him instead of with Guy. How simple it would have been. The thought of Guy obsessed her. She would try to get a few minutes alone in which to telephone him that night.

'I'd hate to see you get involved in his affairs, Anya.'

'What do you mean "affairs"?'

'Well,' Graham explained awkwardly, 'he is married.'

'I'm aware of that.'

'And he was supposed to be pretty cut up when his wife left him.'

The knife went into Anya's heart. 'Was that so unnatural—abnormal?'

'No, but if you saw as much of these marriage triangles as

36

I do, you'd realize the strange quirks that husbands and wives get about each other. They may fight and squabble and say they hate each other, but the habit of being together is stronger than anything else.'

'Is that why there are about 30,000 divorce cases a year?' she flashed.

'No; why there are about treble that number of reconciliations,' he replied flatly.

'I believe Mrs Latimer has been away for about two and a half years.'

'Exactly.'

'What do you mean—exactly?' There was a challenge in Anya's voice.

'That she left him and he hasn't seen her during that time.' Graham was watching her reactions very closely, deliberately provoking her.

'Since that is an established fact why stress it?'

'Because it might be a very different matter if she should return.'

Anya could not conceal the misery within her, or the sick fear his words brought. 'Why should she return?' Her voice was sharp and breathless.

'I was not implying that such a thing was likely—merely wondering what Guy Latimer's reactions would be to that development.'

'Perhaps he would tell you if you asked him,' Anya retorted.

'I doubt very much if he would know.'

Graham's cool incisiveness maddened her, whipping up all the anger that concealed a frantic and destructive emotion.

'I think this conversation is ridiculous.'

'But obviously important to you. Why the defensive attitude otherwise?'

She realized that she must be careful. Once Graham suspected her love for Guy, jealousy might goad him to retaliation. She knew that dangerous gleam in his eyes, that rather thin-lipped expression.

'I was going to ask you that,' she said adroitly.

'My reaction to him is reasonable.' He turned the car into the short drive to Wyvern Close. 'I happen to be in love with you and I can well do without his butting in. 'If I thought . . .' He paused ominously.

'If you thought—what?' Her gaze was challenging, her voice warning.

'Oh, never mind. These married men get on my nerves. Can't make a success of their own lives and do their damnedest to ruin other people's.'

'That is utterly fantastic.'

'Come and sit at my desk for a day and see how fantastic it is. The poor deluded fools of women who always think they are adored. Adored, my foot, they're idiotic playthings who never—for the most part—get beyond the co-respondent stage.'

'Is that the role you have in mind for me?' she snapped.

'It is the role you may well find yourself in.' The car came to a violent standstill. He turned in his seat and put his arm along the back of hers. 'Listen, Anya, your father's worried about you; so am I. All this nonsense about a job when there is no earthly need for you——'

'No earthly need for me to do anything more exciting than be a domestic—here,' she said fiercely. 'I did my job. It's over, Graham. Over. At this moment I'm sick and tired of every brick in my father's house. Call it reaction—anything you like. But nothing will make me change my mind. Anyway, I've taken the plunge. I start tomorrow at The Old Grange Hotel—receptionist.'

Graham gave a disbelieving gasp. Then: 'So that's it . . . the link between you and Latimer. Fawcett and he are old friends.'

'You know about everything, don't you?' She got out of the car.

He joined her almost before she'd taken a step. 'Receptionist,' he said deprecatingly. 'Is that the best you could do?'

'For the time being—yes. Although what's wrong with being a receptionist?'

'Nothing unless *you* happen to be doing it.'

She met his stormy gaze and softened. 'Oh, Graham,' she said with a sigh. 'Please don't you start on me. I've had enough of that.'

'It isn't a question of "starting on you" but of trying to make you see sense.'

'And you think that staying here, going on in this dreary rut is *sense*.'

'No, but marrying me is——'

'Please, Graham,' she begged, 'don't force me to have to hurt you again. I've told you how I feel.'

'But I'd make you love me in the end,' he insisted. 'We've been such good *friends*.'

She sighed. 'I don't want to marry for friendship.' Her voice was gentle.

'Are you in love with *him*?' The words came viciously.

Anya went into the house. She made no attempt to reply.

Marcus Rutherford came to the door of the sitting-room at the sound of footsteps in the hall. Seeing Anya with Graham he beamed.

'So you're together.'

'Yes.' There were times, Graham thought, when Rutherford made some inane remarks.

Anya went into the room ahead of them. She was cold and held her hands out to the fire.

'I've been over to The Old Grange Hotel, Daddy.' She told him the facts and waited for his reactions which, as she had expected, were explosive.

'So you've carried out your threat.'

'Threat? Isn't that rather absurd?'

'No. You're my daughter and I have some position in this

town. *You* taking a job like that, leaving home. I'd far rather you'd gone right out of the district.'

Anya stared at him reflectively. 'You can never see anyone's point of view but your own, can you?'

Marcus looked at Graham. 'Won't she listen to *you*?'

'No,' Graham retorted sullenly.

Daphne sauntered in from the garden, now lying in a soft, purple dusk.

'Hello, Graham. . . . Oh, lord, not another family scrap.' She looked at her father's angry face and then at Anya standing rigid beside the fireplace. It was Graham who explained the position.

Daphne pulled at the waist of her blue cashmere jumper, tightening it over her firm breasts. To Anya's surprise she said: 'Good for you!' Her eyes flashed with sudden challenge as she turned to her father. 'I may as well tell you my plans, too,' she added.

'Your plans,' he echoed weakly.

'I'm going to join forces with Virginia Goodman. She has an exclusive dress shop in Knightsbridge. And a flat that I can share. The money Mummie left me will see me through until I'm worth a salary. I feel like Anya—if I don't get away now I never shall. Sorry, Daddy, but you've had us both with you for far longer than most fathers these days.'

Marcus sagged as he flopped into the nearest chair. He'd envisaged a future in which he and Daphne lived together at Wyvern Close and that even should she marry, she would still make it her home.

'And I don't count—my feelings don't count,' he said icily.

Daphne groaned. 'Oh, for heaven's sake don't let's get on to *that*. If you can't make a new life for yourself . . .' She sighed impatiently. 'It's ridiculous . . . I've managed to find an excellent housekeeper whose coming to see you tomorrow evening. The ideal type. Motherly, plump, physically unattractive, but a Cordon Bleu cook who likes her

40

job and likes to run a house with only a daily to help her.
No one will ever imagine for a second that she is your
mistress! *Very* respectable.'

Marcus's lips were no more than a slit in a mask-like
face. He didn't mind Anya going, except from the point of
view of a lost authority, but Daphne was different. His love
for her was near obsessional.

Anya said gently: 'Change is never pleasant, Daddy—
we all hate it—but this was inevitable. You must have
realized.'

He mumbled weakly: 'Perhaps; but I didn't want to do
so.' He made a helpless gesture. 'It isn't as though you
couldn't have a good time here. Wyvern's such a lovely old
place. . . . I could have the tennis court done for you . . .'
He glanced from face to face, suddenly pathetic, his pom-
pousness and assurance gone as he stood on the edge of a
future unknown, and therefore frightening, to him.

Daphne shot him a look of irritated impatience and
thought, *'Really!'*

Anya's expression was warm and sympathetic.

'Have the tennis court done, Daddy, for when we come
home to visit you. So often people can remain good friends
if they don't live in each other's pockets. If you could see all
this as you would have seen it when you were our age . . . It
isn't because we're hard or indifferent, but because, suddenly, the door of the cage has been opened. After all,
you've shared that cage with us and it is time you escaped
from it too.'

He looked at her gratefully. 'You *will* come to see me?'
His glance strayed uncertainly to Daphne.

'Of course.'

Daphne perched herself on the arm of his chair. Her
attitude changed miraculously. 'Try to get rid of us,' she
exclaimed.

His gaze was anxious. 'Do I know Virginia?'

'Of course you do. We were at school together. You know

41

her father—the old Colonel type. Cheltenham. We used to stay there often.'

'Ah.' He nodded. 'Now I remember.' The old flash of pompous snobbery returned. 'I'm sure his daughter would have the right kind of—of shop.'

Anya tried not to smile, but her eyes met Graham's gaze across the room. She had managed to turn discord into harmony and was glad. But all the time her thoughts were with Guy. Parting from him like that; getting out of his car into Graham's—everything, made her feel bleak and wretched. She muttered some excuse and managed to escape from the room into a small study where the telephone stood on her father's desk. Swiftly and as noiselessly as possible, she made the call, hearing Guy's voice strong and crisp at the other end of the wires.

'I had to ring,' she whispered. 'Darling, I hated leaving like that.'

'And I'm sorry for being such a bore. Did it notice very much?'

'It noticed.' Her heart felt suddenly very light.

'I could have wrung his neck, darling!'

'I'm glad . . . . Guy?'

'Yes.'

'I love you.' She whispered the words and even as she did so saw Daphne standing smirking in the doorway.

4

DAPHNE could never quite understand her feelings for
Anya because they were a mass of contradictions. She knew
that during her mother's illness she had allowed Anya to
take the full burden without offering help of any kind, while
hiding behind a loathing of sickness, maintaining that it
made her ill to watch suffering. Now she was in a position of
hating Anya in many ways because of her own defects. During the past weeks when the running of the household had
been left to her, she had realized what those years must have
meant to Anya—the dreariness, the monotony. And in her
case, there had been no invalid to nurse. The rather mean,
selfish streak within her warred with a natural generosity
and warmth.

'So,' she said and her gaze was sly, 'it's dear Guy, is it?'

Anya hated the knowledge that she could not trust
Daphne, believing that any confidence would automatically
be relayed to their father.

'That is really my business,' she said quietly.

'I should have thought it was his wife's.' Daphne's gaze
was steady and a trifle insolent. 'Funny how the goody-
goody of the family always has a skeleton in the cupboard.
You haven't fooled me for a moment.'

'Meaning?'

'That your virtuous pose of friendship just didn't ring
true.'

Anya took a deep breath, prepared to fight. 'The truth is
very often harder to believe than a skilful lie.'

'Probably. You must be crazy.' She stressed the first

43

syllable of the word. 'What future is there in it? Heck, couldn't you have gone in for something a little more original than that?' She paused significantly. 'I know quite a bit about Guy Latimer.'

Anya mastered the sudden fear that mingled with emotion. 'I'm sure most people do—or think they do. Circumstances like his always provide gossip.'

'I didn't mean that. I met a friend of his wife the other day. She's just come to live in Hereford—a Sylvia March.' Daphne savoured each word. 'Home from Canada. Most interesting.'

Anya's heart missed a beat, but she mastered the overwhelming desire to question precisely what was interesting and said, moving to the door, 'I've no doubt that Mrs Latimer has many friends in this district.'

'If you think he'll ever marry you—you're wrong. He adored Monica, so Mrs March told me, and is always pleading with her to return. . . . Ah, that's something you didn't know—isn't it?'

Anya felt too sick to speak.

Daphne jabbed at what she knew to be a deep wound. 'And this is a sample of what you'll have to put up with in the future if you're fool enough to go on with the man.'

Anya's pride came to her rescue. 'Your solicitude is very touching.'

Daphne flushed. The hurt in Anya's eyes sent a pang through her. 'I'm sorry,' she said and meant it. 'I don't know why I'm such a bitch to you so often. Jealousy, I suppose.'

'*Jealousy!*' Anya spoke as though the idea was fantastic.

'Oh, it's true. But you get in my hair.'

'Why?' Anya's incredulity increased.

'Probably because you used to make me feel so guilty over Mummie.' She added honestly: 'I didn't want to do anything for her myself and resented your doing it.'

'Someone had to take over the responsibility,' Anya said

coolly, trying to forget the searing pain at the thought of Guy and his wife.

'That's it. You took it over. I did not. Conscience, if you like.'

Anya sighed. 'Then for heaven's sake don't pander to it. I certainly don't bear you any grudge over it all. The important thing is that we don't start misunderstanding each other now. . . . I've detested my seemingly efficient, self-sacrificing role—detested it. Not because I minded doing it, but because of being regarded as some little martyr. As you said just now, "goody-goody".' She made a grimace. 'Nauseating. Heaven knows I did my damnedest not to pose as being anything marvellous.'

'You were marvellous all the same. I've only had to run the house and study Daddy's whims and fancies these few weeks to realize it all. . . . I feel better for getting all this off my chest. We could be friends,' she added tentatively.

'We are friends,' Anya corrected.

Daphne's round blue eyes beamed. 'Would you like to marry Guy Latimer?' she asked.

Anya accepted Daphne's appeal without making the mistake of believing that the leopard could change its spots in a second and the distrust remained. Caution prompted her answer.

'I'll tell you if and when the times comes that he is free to marry me.'

Daphne hastened: 'I shan't say anything to Daddy.'

Anya smiled. The promise betrayed the trend of thought.

'He already knows that Guy and I are friends, so there really isn't anything to tell.'

'But if you're in love with each other.' Daphne was dying to know the details.

Anya was intent upon keeping those details secret.

'When there's anything to tell you—anything concrete—I'll do so.' Her voice was pleasant and she managed to infuse a note of lightness.

45

'I can just see Daddy's face if ever you should marry a divorced man. He's frightfully stuffy when it really comes to it.'

Anya shot her a disarming glance. 'And—are you?'

'Don't be funny! I'll probably end up by doing just the same.'

Anya was not deceived. 'Paul Ross?'

Colour flamed into Daphne's cheeks. She spluttered: 'Why—why should you mention him?'

'Because he ties up with Knightsbridge and is Virginia's cousin, and because he has been in Hereford quite a bit lately.'

Daphne's eyes widened in fear. 'How did you know?'

'Are you forgetting our town crier?'

'Mrs Bradstock?'

'Daily women get around. . . . And they have been known to talk,' Anya said drily.

Daphne looked frightened. 'But you——'

'You know I shan't mention it,' Anya said quietly.

Daphne looked shamefaced. Anya was utterly loyal and no further words were necessary.

'Neither shall I,' Anya went on, 'give you any advice. One might just as well tell a person with measles to blow off the rash!'

Daphne heaved a sigh. 'Don't I know it. But every word I said to you was true.'

'That was what convinced me of your feelings for Paul. You were airing your own sub-conscious fears. Perfectly natural.'

'You know people pretty well,' Daphne murmured.

'One breath of experience is worth more than years of theory.'

'Hell, that's true. I resent how I feel, anyway. I get bitter and cynical and I hate him as often as I love him.'

Anya shivered. Would she in time get like that with Guy? Wasn't the spike of fear and mistrust even now churning

46

up every emotion, every suspicion? Did he want his wife back and was *she* only second best, the palliative, never the inspiration, the vital necessity? But as she stood there she remembered the incident of the rooms. . . . Separate rooms. And she heard the echo of his voice saying, '*And now I realize that accepting it before—as I did from the very beginning—proved how very little I knew about love.*' It was as if a great weight lifted from her heart and a calm tinged with happiness stole upon her.

'I suppose that in all these cases the word trust—its degree—is the most vital. Without that who could survive?'

'Put like that it sounds so simple. I trust; you trust, but when you have only words and no actions really to support them, where do you go?'

Anya said solemnly: 'Just as far away from the man as is possible. One might just as well crucify oneself as remain to be crucified and to lose all one's self respect.'

Daphne almost threw the question at her. 'And would you have that amount of courage?'

Anya was trembling as she answered: 'I believe I would. Proof of disloyalty, of bad faith. . . .' She shook her head.

'Ah—*proof.*' Daphne's eyes narrowed, becoming slits in her pale, doll-like face. 'And if proof were impossible to get?'

Anya's expression was rueful. 'No relationship on earth can go on indefinitely if it is based on lies. Sooner or later truth wins.'

Daphne nodded. 'And one can dread even that.'

Anya stared at her. She had thought in terms of a mild flirtation where Paul was concerned, with Daphne flattered, for Paul was a prominent figure in the literary world and his last book had been something of a best seller. Now she realized that the association was much deeper and more serious, and that when it came to emotional reactions human beings were strangers even to those most intimately connected with them. Genuine concern, affection, a curious

47

sensation of responsibility forced her to ask: 'Do you really think going to London is the best thing for you?'

Daphne answered that by saying: 'And do you think that going to The Old Grange is the best thing for you?'

Anya did not need to speak.

'You see?' Daphne's voice held a note of desperation. 'Every time I arrange to meet Paul I'm determined to end things.' Her laugh was ironical. 'And he's only to look at me, to touch me and I'm sunk. No character—that's my trouble.'

'Then half the people in the world share that handicap,' Anya retorted. Her gaze deepened and a protective instinct stirred within her. She had no desire to pry, ready to give the same privacy as she herself demanded in her own relationship, but she said gently, 'If you are not getting any happiness——'

'I could be happy. I *could*. . . . He's going to America at the end of the year. He and his wife don't get on; his plans are to leave her for good then.'

'Will she divorce him?'

'He says she will.'

Anya could *feel* the agony of doubt behind the words.

'And he would marry you?'

'Yes. . . . But so much can happen between now and the end of the year, Anya. It's the suspense. I've been happy until these past weeks. Somehow I don't think he really wants me to go to London—to be nearer him.'

'That may be for your own protection.'

'I suppose so.'

'What does Virginia say?'

'She doesn't know. My joining forces with her . . . Well, she really wanted someone. I should have gone to London in any case. Paul says he will tell her in his own time. She and his wife don't get on, apparently. That should help.' Her expression changed, her mood lightened. 'It's a relief to talk about it.'

48

The depression crept back as Anya dwelt again on her own problem. Sylvia March. . . . She found herself asking urgently: 'Daphne, were you telling the truth just now—about what Mrs March said?'

Daphne didn't hesitate. 'Yes,' she said, her voice low. 'It was a beastly thing to repeat, anyway.'

'What sort of woman is Mrs March?'

'Very smart. Her husband is a Captain in the navy. She is staying here with her parents while he goes off on some mission or other. I met her when I was having coffee with Elaine. I don't remember just how the subject of the Latimers came up. Oh, yes, I know: Mrs March said that she'd been staying with Monica in Montreal. I pumped her, to be honest.'

'I see,' said Anya, misery washing over her as suspicion crept back.

They returned to the sitting-room. Graham looked from face to face, disgruntled and irritated by Anya's long absence.

'I was just coming to look for you,' he said tartly. 'Will you have dinner with me, Anya?'

'I'm sorry, Graham, but I've quite a bit to do—getting ready for tomorrow. Packing, sorting. I'm sure you understand.'

'I understand that any excuse is better than none.'

Marcus looked at Anya reprovingly. *Why* couldn't she realize Graham's good qualities; why couldn't she marry him? It would be an ideal arrangement. Eventually, Graham would take over the firm and he, Marcus, would feel that whatever happened Daphne and Anya would be secure, for he had no doubt of Graham's integrity.

Anya was in no mood for argument. Every word being uttered was merely superimposed on the screen of her real and turbulent thoughts, her acute depression. She shrank from the aching distrust within her heart, from the agony of conflict about Guy's feelings for her, and yet was loath to

49

make an issue of gossip, or to betray her own lack of confidence.

'I'm sorry,' she said firmly, 'if you feel like that, you must.'

Graham was too much one of the family to hide his annoyance. 'I suppose if it were Latimer you'd manage to accept the invitation *and* get your packing done.'

Marcus flashed Anya a challenging, suspicious glance, then turned to Graham at whom Anya was gazing in faint contempt.

'What's all this?' he demanded.

Graham instantly retreated. The last thing he wished to do was to stir up any trouble for Anya. 'Nothing more important than my own damned jealousy—quite unfounded,' he admitted gallantly.

Anya's animosity vanished before that evidence of loyalty.

'If we could be back here at about ten-thirty, I'd like to have dinner with you,' she murmured, remembering Graham's devotion and appreciating it.

He brightened. 'We'll run in to The Green Dragon.'

But there was only one thought in Anya's mind throughout the rest of that evening—to talk to Guy, to convince herself of his sincerity.

Graham said gently, as they sat over their coffee after dinner—having chosen a deserted corner of the hotel lounge: 'You're unhappy tonight—what is it? Oh, I know I'm difficult and jealous, but I do *care*.'

She said bleakly: 'And it isn't that I don't value your concern for me, Graham. Why has life to be such a muddle?'

'So you admit yours is a muddle,' he said, his attitude instantly changing.

'I was thinking,' she answered honestly, 'of why we couldn't love to order. 'Doesn't that make life a muddle?'

He muttered grudgingly: 'I suppose so. I'd be almost happy if I could convince myself that Latimer wasn't in the picture.' He saw the flashing resistance of her expression and added: 'Oh, all right—I won't harp on the subject, but promise me that if ever you want me—in any capacity— you'll come to me and not shut me out. That hurts, Anya.'

She put out a hand and touched his. 'I promise. . . . You're far too good for me. I just don't know why you bother.'

He smiled. 'Probably because life *is* such a muddle.'

'Exactly,' she agreed.

'But you still won't confide in me.' His voice was bitter.

'When I have anything concrete to tell, you shall be the first to know.'

And with that he had to be content.

5

ANYA and Guy met at Brockhampton the following morning. Anya had telephoned him and made the appointment,
hiring a car to take her the eight miles out of Hereford. She
knew she could not start any new and unfamiliar job with
her mind in turmoil and suspicion blinding her to reason.

At a spot near the thatched lychgate of the picturesque
old church she dismissed the car, paid the driver and explained that she would get a 'bus back. Guy drove up in that
second, swung out of the driving seat and strode anxiously
towards her.

'Darling, what's wrong?' He studied her intently, watching the hire car drive away down the familiar lane. 'I
dropped everything after you telephoned. You sounded
so odd.'

There were butterflies in her stomach and a weight seeming to press on her heart as she looked at him and panicked.
This might well be the end, she told herself desperately, and
then drawing on her courage said quietly: 'I must talk to
you, Guy. Let's sit in the car.'

They moved towards it and Anya never forgot that
moment when all the peace and glory of the spring morning
mocked her.

'Now,' he demanded urgently, when they were settled in
their seats.

She let the words tumble out, catching her breath, her
eyes wide and frightened in their appeal as she asked: 'Did
you—do you—love Monica so much that you've done
everything to get her back?'

He puckered his brows and faced her steadily.

'That rather depends on what you mean by everything.' His voice hardened. 'And either you trust me, Anya, or you don't.'

'It isn't a question of trust,' she said, feeling sick with unhappiness.

'Then what is it? And why, after last evening, talk like this? Something must have happened.' His gaze was unnerving. 'That probably means gossip. . . . Suppose you tell me the facts so that I can deal with them.'

She did so, watching him with avid concern, hanging on his answer. He sat there outwardly calm, almost expressionless. Then: 'Sylvia March,' he echoed. 'So she's in Hereford.'

Anya felt the colour rising in her cheeks, there was something in his attitude that made her feel at a disadvantage.

'Listen, Guy,' she rushed on, 'don't misunderstand me, it is just that I couldn't bear it if in your heart you wanted your wife back. Oh, I know what you've said, but impulse, loneliness can play their part.'

'And do you imagine, if that were so, I should have asked you to marry me when I'm free, or even to want a divorce? Does it occur to you that I'd have thought in terms of being your lover rather than your future husband?'

'I appreciate that, but——'

'You want a categorical denial that I've tried to get her back?'

Anya cried: 'I want to know how you feel—in your heart.'

His stillness was unnerving, his expression seemingly emotionless. 'I want my freedom. I am not in love with Monica, but with you. On one occasion—soon after she left —I did write to her to see if we couldn't patch things up and start again. That *was* an impulse, and I was thankful when she didn't reply.'

Anya said weakly: 'Oh, *Guy* . . . I know I've been a fool.

But'—her eyes grew suspiciously bright—'somehow I couldn't bear it.'

He put his arm around her shoulders and kissed the side of her head, pressing her against him, soothing her as though she were a child.

'Satisfied?' A whimsical teasing note crept into his voice.

She sighed—a deep sigh of relief.

'I imagine it was Sylvia who telephoned the farm.' Guy spoke with a certain curiosity.

'You know her very well?'

'Too well. She's dangerous because no one ever suspects it, and I don't think she quite realizes herself just what trouble she can make for people.' He chuckled. 'You— *child*.'

She nodded her head in agreement, but her eyes sparkled. 'I know,' she said in a little apologetic voice.

'Let this be a lesson to you. Want my wife back,' he repeated scornfully. 'If you knew how petrified I am in case anything should go wrong.' His arms tightened around her. 'Darling, please understand and never be so foolish again.'

'I do understand and I promise.'

'There's bound to be gossip. People love distortion and trouble making. They like the limelight of juggling with the happiness of others.'

'That sounds dreadful.'

'It is, but true of some types. The important thing is that we have faith in each other. Without that, Anya, it would be quite hopeless.' His expression hardened. 'I couldn't stand mistrust, suspicion.'

Anya felt small. But the circumstances were foreign to her, what was more, having lived so long at Wyvern in an atmosphere of protection as well as restriction, she had not yet accustomed herself to the impact of freedom and its attendant responsibilities, any more than she had made the necessary emotional adjustment. Love, desire, hope, the

54

future had made an onslaught upon her, sensitizing her beyond the normal limits, and with these walked fear.

'I won't transgress again,' she said solemnly.

He held her gaze masterfully. 'No, my darling, please don't.'

They sat there, the sun rifting through the car windows and throwing a mosaic upon road and hedgerow. Around them apple blossom, lilacs, poured out their fragrance into the warmth of the blue and gold day. The sound of a lawn mower did nothing to break the silence, but rather merged into it.

'I must get back,' Anya said regretfully.

'I'll run you home.'

'No, I——'

'I'll run you home,' he repeated firmly.

She shot him a whimsical glance. 'Stubborn?'

'I shall have to be with you!'

'I rather like the idea of being told what to do. I've looked after other people for so long that just to relax—wonderful! Oh, Guy,' she whispered tensely, 'I must make you happy; be everything you want, and need.'

His gaze was deep and tender. 'You do, and you are, darling.'

She leaned towards him and he kissed her swiftly.

'I've interrupted your work,' she commented ruefully as they drove back to Hereford.

'You have,' he agreed with a chuckle. 'What are you going to do about it?'

'Would "I love you" help?'

He took her hand and pressed it against his cheek.

Anya's heart sang with the day. Happiness poured over her almost as though it were a measurable sensation. The muscles of her throat contracted making her catch at her breath. With Guy beside her everything was so right, so simple, and her own former suspicions and fears fantastic and an insult to him.

'I shall come over to the hotel to see you,' he said as they neared Hereford. 'Jimmy will neither question nor comment.'

'And the staff, the guests?'

'They will assume I come over to visit him.' His laughter was throaty. 'That's my story and I'm sticking to it. There are many places, anyway, around the district where we can meet. I think it would be better if you rang me, darling.'

Anya smiled. 'I'd love that. Women hate waiting for the telephone calls that men hate making!'

'I don't hate making them to you.' He looked irritated. 'I wish I could stay and take you over to The Grange this afternoon.'

'No.' She spoke with emphasis. 'That would not be wise, darling. Daddy's going to run me there, anyway.'

'He's reconciled to it?'

'Not exactly that, but the softening process has started. My sister's going away, too, and he will have to make some kind of a life for himself. The hardest, but the kindest way. We've never been close, but I think we may come to understand each other in the end. He and my mother were never suited—quite apart from her illness. Marriage can be so bleak, so empty without companionship, or any mutual interests. Daddy was so remote from her.'

It was just as they reached the bridge that, caught in a traffic jam, Anya saw a woman waving frantically to Guy as she stood close to them on the pavement.

'Good lord—Sylvia March,' he groaned. 'Nothing we can do about it, except stop at the spot she's indicating lower down where I can park.'

It was the last thing Anya wanted. The idea of knowing any of Monica's friends crashed into her bright new world superimposing the past on both present and future, and giving Monica substance.

The car stopped. She and Guy got out. Guy made the introductions.

Sylvia, elegant in her short, tight skirt and loose, grey tweed jacket with its banana silk scarf knotted at the neck, said: 'I telephoned you, Guy . . . I was going to do so again. Only been back a few days. . . . It's wonderful to see you.' She slurred her words into a rather affected drawl and then, looking at Anya with faint suspicion, said: 'Rutherford. . . . Surely I met someone of that name the other morning?'

'My sister perhaps,' Anya suggested cautiously.

'With Elaine Morgan?'

'Yes.'

Sylvia eyed Anya with a hawk-like stare. Just where did she fit into Guy's life? In turn, Anya decided that she definitely did not like this woman with her heavy make-up, eye-shadow and rather cruel mouth—a vivid red gash in a rougeless face. There was something predatory and sly about her. She stood there almost challengingly so that Anya was left with the feeling that she herself had a secret to hide. In some subtle fashion Sylvia March brought Monica actively to life as she said slowly and with deliberation: 'By the way, I saw Monica just before I left. She told me to look you up.'

Guy felt that every nerve in his body had tightened. He shrank from the knowledge that Sylvia's words could not fail to hurt Anya, even to make her uneasy.

'Really,' he said almost curtly.

Sylvia's gaze travelled with insolent leisureliness from Guy's face to Anya. Her own mood was truculent and it helped to vent it upon others.

'I really don't blame you for still carrying the torch, my dear man. Monica's that kind of woman. Men just can't resist her helplessness. It flatters their conceit, I suppose.' Her laughter was shrill. 'But it is *so* good to see you again. We simply *must* get together. I've so much to tell you—messages and all that, far too personal to pass on as we stand here like this. I want to make you understand about Monica, too.'

'I understand already,' Guy said tartly.

She smiled knowingly. 'You only think you do. . . .'

Anya watched Guy with an agonizing intensity. What was he feeling? What were his reactions to the subtle innuendo of those words and where would they lead? He spoke lightly in reply: 'I don't even think, Sylvia. One has to be sufficiently interested before that is applicable.'

There was a crafty look in her eyes as she studied him.

'I should take a great deal of convincing to believe that your interest had really died, Guy. You're the loyal type. I admire that—particularly in a man—don't you, Miss Rutherford?'

Anya beat down a rising anger and managed to say calmly: 'Very much, but the word can be greatly abused or misinterpreted.' She knew even as she spoke that she had made an indiscreet remark which Sylvia March instantly seized upon.

'Meaning that I have misinterpreted Guy's loyalty?'

Anya forced a faintly amused smile. 'I think this has become rather an odd conversation between strangers, Mrs March. I am in no position to answer your question, or to understand your remarks.'

Sylvia smirked. 'No,' she said with a lingering insolence, 'that's true.'

Guy, furious, tried to keep his temper, but the tone of his voice was icy. 'If you'll excuse us . . . I've to get back to work.'

'I'll ring you,' Sylvia said confidently. 'Or perhaps we could arrange to have dinner. Are you free tomorrow night?'

'Without looking at my diary I can't possibly say.'

'The social type these days—eh?'

'How is your husband?' he countered.

'Very well—when last I heard. He's gone to some God-forsaken-place, vilely hot. Not for me,' she added. 'I detest the heat.'

'Then,' said Anya, 'you should be blissfully happy in England.'

They parted and Guy said angrily: 'I never could stand

that woman.' He shot Anya a meaning glance. 'Now perhaps you can realize what a trouble maker she is and could
be.'

'I realize,' Anya agreed.

'I shall certainly not have dinner with her or, for that
matter, meet her at any time. I couldn't start an argument in
the street or I'd have told her so. She's one of those un-
pleasant people who would stop at nothing to gain her own
ends—the interfering type.'

'Obviously very close to—to——'

'Monica,' he put in quietly. 'Yes, although I doubt very
much if she is capable of being the friend of anyone.' There
was an earnest, anxious note in his voice as he added: 'These
next months are going to be a lifetime of suspense for me.'

'Suspense?'

'Until I am really *free*.'

Anya felt a wave of emotion, of tenderness surge over her.
'So long as we have each other the waiting will be bearable,
darling.'

Guy nearly hit the car in front of him as his brakes
screeched.

'If only I could hold up the traffic and kiss you for that!'

'I'd better not dare you,' she retorted, suddenly gay. 'And
I'm afraid it's time for you to drop me—over there, near
the chemist.'

He said firmly: 'I'm taking you to the door, darling. The
idea of any secrecy now that we've seen Sylvia is ridiculous.'

'I hadn't thought of that.'

Guy looked angry. Sylvia was representative of everything he most disliked in a woman and he had always resented and distrusted her. She brought back a depression
that he could not overcome. Her glib references to Monica,
her innuendo, irritated him, the more so because it placed
him at a disadvantage. His love for Anya had become a deep
and integral part of his life, and the possibility that she might
be hurt, or that she might well misunderstand Sylvia's

distortions, brought an uneasiness and a fear. At this stage he could not protect her by any public declaration of his true feelings, and he loathed the secrecy imposed upon him by circumstances.

The car stopped at Wyvern Close. Anya said gently: 'Thank you, Guy—for everything. Most of all for understanding my stupid behaviour.'

He held her gaze steadfastly. 'I can put myself in your chair, darling. Only *please* never think the wrong thing and' —he paused significantly—'trust me. I love you, Anya. Those words embrace everything and are my answer—always.'

She didn't speak, just stood there looking at him, feeling the glow of his words, the excitement of his nearness and his steady, adoring gaze. There was nothing to worry about— nothing. All the Sylvias in the world could not part them unless they wished it so. He was right. Only trust and love mattered.

Their hands touched, clung and fell apart.

'No, don't get out of the car,' she murmured.

'Ring me tonight.' His voice was low.

'I will.'

'And I'll come over in a day or so.' A smile transformed his face. 'That means tomorrow.'

'I hoped it might.' She glanced about her. 'I must rush now.' As she spoke she slipped from her seat, shut the car door, threw an adoring glance at him over her shoulder and disappeared into the drive-way.

Daphne saw her from the landing window and was in the hall to greet her. 'Out early,' she said.

Anya flushed.

'The boy friend.' Daphne perched herself on the edge of the heavy Jacobean oak settle. She looked pleased with life. 'Paul rang me just now. He's meeting me in London on Friday and taking me over to Virginia's flat.'

'Please,' Anya said suddenly, almost involuntarily, 'don't

rush into anything, Daphne. Oh, it's not for me to give advice, or even express an opinion——'

'You said that last night,' Daphne reminded her.

'I know.' Anya felt helpless and inadequate.

'And it's too late, anyway,' Daphne went on, and her gaze was tentative. 'You may just as well know.'

The breathlessness in Anya's voice betrayed emotion rather than solicitude, 'You mean——'

'We've been lovers for two months.'

'Oh.'

Daphne slid off the settle and stretched herself, staring at Anya quizzically.

'And if you're honest, you and Guy Latimer are, too.'

Anya's heart raced, the thought constituting desire.

'No.' Her voice was quiet and without a hint of virtue. 'As a matter of fact we're not.'

'You will be,' came the confident retort. 'I began with all the best intentions, but emotion destroys them all in the end. . . . Don't really know why I've told you; possibly because the thrill of it seems more real when someone understands the position. I've been pretty tired of playing the innocent young girl role I might tell you, and listening to Daddy's pious drivel.'

'Is Paul still going to America?'

'Of course.' Daphne spoke sharply. 'I told you he was. His work can't stop for that reason. . . . My visits to Ledbury to see Renee have been pretty convenient. . . . Weren't you ever suspicious?'

Anya knew then that she had been, but her own problems had made it easy for her to hide the fact from herself.

'I wondered if there might be someone.' Anya sighed. 'I'm afraid we weren't close enough for discussion.' Anxiety betrayed itself in her expression. 'I'm worried about you now. So much could happen in a situation like that.'

'I could become pregnant for instance.' Daphne's voice was a trifle defiant.

'It's a risk—a dangerous risk.'

'It might not be such a bad thing,' Daphne said darkly.

Anya gasped. 'But how could that possibly help?'

'By bringing everything to a head. There'd have to be a divorce quickly then.'

Anya saw then that despite the apparent sophistication, the worldliness, Daphne was still completely immature— the greedy child wanting its own way and blind to all the obstacles.

'And suppose it had just the opposite effect? Suppose there should be no divorce? Would it be so very——'

Daphne burst out: 'Paul would never let me down.' Colour mounted her cheeks as she remembered all she had said only the previous evening—of the fears she had voiced about the future and the cynicism embellishing those fears.

'All the same, don't take risks; don't deliberately delude yourself.'

'I was just talking foolishly—recklessly,' Daphne admitted. 'I wanted your reactions.'

'My reactions are concerned with your happiness, your future.'

'I believe that. I haven't any happiness—or future— without Paul.'

Anya disliked the thought that flashed into her mind just then as she asked if it might not be the thrill and excitement of a forbidden association which constituted the greatest attraction for Daphne—that and Paul's success as a writer. And as if reading her thoughts, Daphne challenged: 'You don't think I'm sincere, do you?'

Anya said quietly: 'Perhaps for your sake I could wish you weren't. I don't want to see you hurt.'

'But you're not afraid of being hurt—or are you?' Daphne's eyes flashed as she spoke.

'We were not talking of me. . . . And I must get changed. It's almost one.'

As she spoke Marcus Rutherford let himself in at the front door.

Daphne stared at him. 'You're early.'

Anya began to mount the stairs, pausing as Marcus said: 'Anya, I'm sorry, but Graham will have to run you over to the hotel this afternoon. I've an important client to see unexpectedly. Can't avoid it. But Graham certainly won't be sorry to take my place and accompany you.'

Anya looked upset. She didn't want Graham to drive her to The Old Grange, particularly as Guy believed she was being driven there by her father.

'I can get a 'bus,' she said.

'Nonsense.' Marcus spoke sharply. 'It would be ungracious and unnecessary, apart from the fact that you've forgotten your baggage.'

'Of course; you're quite right,' she agreed.

Marcus brightened. 'I'll drive over to see you from time to time,' he said affably, trying to overcome the depression that had settled upon him at the realization that soon he would be alone at Wyvern—apart from the housekeeper Daphne had introduced into the scheme of things, and whom he had yet to see and approve.

Anya tried to sound enthusiastic. 'That would be lovely.' Her words echoed hollowly through the silent house.

'I can't quite believe you're both going,' Marcus said unsteadily. He looked at Daphne reproachfully. 'London! I'll never understand that. You've lived so differently all your life. Doesn't make sense to me.'

Daphne flashed him an irritable glance.

'Oh, Daddy! Don't start all that again—please!'

Anya changed the subject swiftly. 'What time is Graham picking me up?'

'At two o'clock.'

'Then I must get changed. . . . Mrs Bradstock is getting the meal I believe.'

Daphne said shortly: 'She certainly is. I've done all the cooking I ever want to do, believe me.'

Anya went to her bedroom and for a second sat down at her dressing-table. It seemed many years since her mother's death and the pattern of her life became suddenly unreal. She was taking a job which involved responsibility outside the isolated walls of that house. For a moment she panicked. Her typing and shorthand were by no means speedy because she had taken the course before her mother's illness and practised only rarely. Languages were different. She had kept them up by reading books in both German and French. The only consolation was that the typing and shorthand could be polished up as she went along—if indeed she should require them, although it was pretty obvious that hers would not be the true-to-type receptionist job. A smile touched her lips. James Fawcett had made that pretty clear and, in the end, the fact might tell in her favour.

There came that last moment when she faced her father in the dining-room to say good-bye and she knew that he realized a chapter at Wyvern was being ended. The sadness lay in the truth that she would not miss him, and that he had been a ghost in her life rather than a vitalizing influence.

'Good-bye, Anya.' He was amazed how little real emotion he felt and how philosophical he had suddenly become. The possibility of his own future took shape furtively at the back of his mind. Re-marriage. . . . The idea excited him as a dormant sex urge began to awaken. He was free and with Anya and Daphne away . . . The blood in his veins heated. Was *he* thinking like that? Daphne, whom he had built his life around. . . . Yet even as he stood there he had a vision of a woman in an absurd, nonsensical hat whose eyes had met his in provocative challenge. . . . Loreli Fairfax whom he had known for two years and pretended to regard only as a client—without quite succeeding.

Watching him, Anya felt the impact of some new element which made her realize that he had already made friends

64

with circumstance, and even though it may have gone no further than ceasing to deceive himself about his feelings, it was a step in the right direction.

'Good-bye, Daddy. Be happy. Get out all you can.' Her gaze met his meaningly: 'And think about providing us with a stepmother.'

He gave her a rather sickly smile, but without making any protest or betraying resentment at the suggestion.

'I can hear Graham's car,' he hastened.

Anya paused by Daphne's side.

'Take care,' she whispered, 'and keep in touch—*please*.'

'I will.' Daphne leaned forward and kissed Anya's cheek. 'And thanks for all you've done over the years.'

Coming from her it was almost an illuminated address.

6

AFTER a few weeks at The Old Grange, Anya felt she had lived there for years. There was a friendliness in the atmosphere and the staff accepted her rather as a member of a family. James Fawcett was precisely as she imagined he would be—kindly, considerate, volatile and progressive. Una Colby, his secretary, was true to her earlier promise and showed Anya 'the ropes', encouraging her and making it simple for her to familiarize herself with the work which was, even as James Fawcett had warned her, comprehensive! Anya loved her comfortable room which, on the third floor, overlooked the panorama of Herefordshire and Monmouthshire, missing most of the actual grounds of the hotel itself. At last, she told herself, she had become an individual. As she sat in the reception cubicle—more spacious than most—with the plan of the rooms spread out before her, she felt that she was looking through the window of the world. The guests were varied, ranging from Cabinet ministers and film stars to the modest family man. There were those who barked their orders, making up in arrogance and pomposity for that which they lacked in breeding, and those who gave instructions with a smile, making any service given in exchange a privilege. The intricacies of bookings, of cancellations, of those who on arrival at the hotel wanted the accommodation changed completely—all this became simple once she had mastered the art of juggling in order to please everyone.

Una Colby, looking at her after those first weeks, said warmly: 'You've honestly done wonders, my dear.

Heavens, how we've suffered from nitwits! Happy here?'

'Wonderfully,' said Anya, and it was true.

'Anyone special coming in today?'

'Yes, Dodie Martin, the actress, and a Mr Lance Vimore.'

'The boy friend. One double and one single?'

Anya laughed. 'That's it. She went into a long explanation as to why she couldn't possibly sleep in a single bed!'

'Ah, the fishy ones always *explain*. As if we cared! We're here to let rooms, not to interest ourselves in morals, and we can hardly ask for marriage certificates! That couple in number eight would be hard pressed if we did.'

'Mr and Mrs Wynton?' Anya looked disbelieving.

'Yes.'

'But, they're charming people.' Anya hastened awkwardly. 'I didn't mean to put it like that as though——'

'I know exactly what you mean . . . but it sticks out a mile. They're so happy, but watch her off guard.'

Anya shivered. 'Sadness?'

'Exactly. He's married unless my name isn't Una Colby. A genuine couple I'd say. Caught up in some misery. I've seen it too many times not to recognize it.'

Anya lowered her gaze from Una Colby's searching one. Then she said explosively: 'Life seems so—so absurd. The happy people not allowed to be together and the incompatibles stuck together like glue.'

'The façade of marriage. Inevitable, I suppose. Loathe it myself.' Una Colby spoke as she typed, her words like machine-gun fire. 'Now you take that Wesmore couple. Been coming here for years. Hardly ever say a word to each other. He looks so bored he could jump in the river and she natters perpetually—to anyone unfortunate enough to be within listening radius—probably to prevent herself bursting into tears.'

Anya wasn't concentrating on anything being said, she was thinking that she would be seeing Guy that evening.

'Do you,' she asked irrelevantly, 'know a Mrs Mortimer?'

67

She was studying the plan as she spoke. 'She's coming down from London this afternoon. The booking was made by a friend.'

'Mortimer. A pretty common name, but I think she's a new one.'

James Fawcett strode into the reception cubicle which opened into a larger office where Una Colby sat typing.

'The 15th August,' he said, looking at Anya. 'Hospital Ball. Research charity. They want covers for a hundred at least. Hell, the place will be alive with people.' He sighed. 'But if we don't cope——'

Anya said swiftly: 'Why not use the games room for dinner—it could be transformed with flowers—you couldn't add a hundred diners to those already staying in the hotel and we're booked solidly in August. I suppose you can hire tables and chairs.'

Una Colby got up from her desk. 'It's an idea you know, Mr Fawcett.'

'It is, by jove. And I know who'll help me out with the hire stuff. Anya, you're a wizard. I've been tearing my hair —what's left to tear,' he added comically, for he was prematurely thinning on top. 'I'd come to the conclusion that we'd have to use the ballroom for dinner and clear it afterwards, but it's pretty grim. . . . The games room.' He chuckled. 'That'll put some noses out of joint among the table tennis enthusiasts.'

'We should worry,' said Una Colby bluntly. 'One night won't kill 'em.'

'Pity,' said James Fawcett.

'And can I do the flowers?' Anya asked.

'Can you?' He expanded. 'I'll say you can!'

They laughed together and he perched himself on the arm of a heavy oak chair near Anya's desk, looking at her speculatively.

She smiled at him. 'Mr Goolman was asking to see you just now.'

'Dick? Oh! That means that his wife wants one or two waiters sacked! She's a shocker, drives me and him—poor devil—insane. I think she's sat at every table in the dining-room during this holiday and none is ever right.'

'Then why does she come here?' Anya asked, amazed.

'Probably because she wouldn't be tolerated anywhere else! She's been thrown out of most restaurants and hotels as it is. I like Dick, therefore I put up with her.'

'Why does he?' Anya inquired.

'Heaven knows.' He took a deep breath. 'Marriage seems to make some men like rabbits in the power of a stoat. Lose all resistance.

Una Colby added to that. 'Men have no moral courage whatsoever when it comes to women—a trite but true observation.'

James Fawcett chuckled and left them. Una Colby returned to her typewriter, Anya went on with her booking.

It was just before three o'clock that Mrs Mortimer arrived. Anya watched her as she came through the swing doors and walked up to the reception desk.

Una Colby said appreciatively: 'Hm-m. Now that's what I call a pretty woman. Bet she's either a widow or an ex.'

'Ex?' Anya looked puzzled.

'Ex-wife, divorcee.'

'Oh.'

The fragrance of an expensive scent reached them before its wearer, then: 'A friend booked a room for me. . . .'

'Mrs Mortimer?'

'Yes.'

Anya said pleasantly: 'Room Ten with a private bath. For one week.'

'I may stay on.'

Anya met a steady gaze from china-blue eyes that were wide and disarming. She *was* pretty, with fair hair and a pale, seemingly transparent skin, very fine. Her clothes were simple but obviously expensive.

69

'I'm afraid number ten is let next week, Mrs Mortimer—the day you are due to vacate it.'

'Couldn't you switch things a bit?' The smile was sweet but it held resistance to opposition.

'I'm afraid not for that particular room. It is a regular booking, but we can easily move you to an equally good one.'

'Oh well, I suppose that will have to do, then.'

Anya rotated the register and waited for it to be signed.

'I've just returned from Canada,' Mrs Mortimer said casually, as she wrote her address. 'I haven't a home in England at the moment.'

Canada! Anya could not help the sudden sickness that came upon her. The word was bound up so vitally with her future that it could not fail to have significance.

'Canada,' she echoed rather breathlessly.

Mrs Mortimer eyed her with curiosity. 'You give it importance.'

'One hears so much about it,' Anya hastened.

'A magnificent country . . . but one can get home-sick.' She studied Anya intently and her gaze was unnerving.

'I've not had the good fortune to travel,' Anya murmured, 'so I wouldn't know.'

'And I was determined to do so,' came the friendly comment. 'Probably far too determined. Roots can be valuable.' She added with a half smile: 'When one has torn them up.'

Anya stood there feeling almost deflated as she watched the porter lead Mrs Mortimer towards the lift. Anything that reminded her of the fact that Guy was married plunged a knife into her heart and it was useless pretending otherwise.

She worked until six, changed into a cool cotton dress and was about to leave the hotel to meet Guy at their appointed spot when he came towards her, greeting her just a little too casually in an effort to convey mere friendliness.

70

'I was just——' She stopped.

He hastened before she could finish: 'I had to see Jimmy so I thought it would be permissible to call for you and have a drink here, darling.' The endearment slipped out and they smiled into each other's eyes.

James Fawcett appeared in the doorway of his office.

'Hello there, Guy! I've been trying to get in touch with you.'

'I got your message and here I am.'

'Trying to undermine Anya's loyalty,' came the whimsical retort. 'None of it, old boy. She's absolutely indispensable.'

'I can well believe that. . . . Don't forget I recommended her!'

'I won't. . . . You must both have a drink with me.' He beckoned a waiter and gave the order, having consulted them as to their choice. 'We might as well sit on the terrace —cooler there.' His gaze rested upon Anya. 'You were going into Cinderford, weren't you? I was about to suggest running you there.'

Guy said firmly: 'I shall be calling at a farm there and can easily give Anya a lift.'

'Rivalry,' James said with a grin.

The two men exchanged glances. James was not deceived.

'Hotel full?' Guy asked, as a little later they sat together on the terrace sipping their drinks and looking out over the shady lawns and tall beech trees which formed almost an avenue down to the river.

'Only a few rooms empty. I'm pretty delighted.'

It was in that moment that Mrs Mortimer stepped out of the drawing-room, pausing almost as if aware of her own fascination, in order that they might take in every detail of her slim-fitting, dazzlingly white gown, with which she wore as her only ornament a diamond shoulder spray. Her fair hair had a polished look about it and her make-up was as

71

discreet as her skin was flawless. She wasn't, Anya decided, the *femme fatale*, but rather the deceptively innocent appealing type who looked towards them and then gave a little breathless gasp.

'My God,' cried James.

'*Monica!*'

Anya heard that name on Guy's lips almost as a death knell, seeing his face pale, his eyes darken in a staggered expression of utter disbelief.

Mrs Mortimer!

Both men got to their feet as Monica moved towards them. She was quiet and poised as she said: 'Hello, Guy . . . Jimmy. It's good to see you again.' Her gaze swept beyond them to Anya. 'I registered under my maiden name.' Her smile was slow and secretive and it sent a shudder over Anya's body.

James came to the rescue by introducing Anya after which came an awkward silence. Monica broke it by saying pleasantly: 'May I join you?' She sat down even as she asked the question.

Every emotion from fear to an angry desperation possessed Guy as he watched her. What did she want? Why was she there? He looked at Anya imploringly, willing her to understand both his desperation and his desolation and knowing, with a sick sensation of inevitability, that it was almost impossible for her to appreciate either.

'Why,' he demanded almost curtly, 'are you in England?'

Her expression changed, becoming a little sad.

'Guy, I was going to ring you. . . . Jimmy, you've not altered a scrap. . . . This is a lovely old place.'

'How—how did you know about it?' James was trying to fathom Guy's reactions, to decide just what kind of impact Monica had made.

'From a friend of mine.'

'Sylvia March,' Guy said shortly. 'I saw her in Hereford a few weeks ago.'

72

Monica smiled. It was, in truth, a habit, rather than a reflection of her feelings or her thoughts.

'Yes. Sylvia kept me informed. She's a wonderful letter writer.' Monica paused. 'How's Green Meadows? You know it seems many years since I lived there.'

'It is many years,' he retorted.

'Two and a half hardly rate that description, although I agree that one cannot measure anything in actual time.'

Anya got to her feet. She could not endure it another second. 'If you'll excuse me,' she said coolly without looking at Guy, 'I have an appointment.'

'I'm afraid I've rather butted in,' Monica murmured.

James took his place by Anya's side.

'You must forgive us . . . work. . . . I'll see you later.'

Guy's voice fell almost harshly upon the momentary silence.

'Good-bye, Monica,' he said with emphasis.

Anya's heart missed a beat.

Monica looked up at him. 'I've come all the way from Canada to talk to you,' she said gently. 'If you are busy now, I'll come to the farm tomorrow.'

James and Anya moved swiftly away. Guy answered almost despairingly: 'We've nothing to talk about, Monica. Nothing. You chose your way of life and now I have decided upon mine. Let's leave it at that.'

He felt her gaze pleadingly, appealingly upon him.

'It still wouldn't change if you were to listen to what I have to say. After all you cannot wipe out a marriage by pretending it doesn't exist. . . . Would eleven o'clock tomorrow suit you?'

Just then the overwhelming, the overpowering desire within Guy's heart was to get to Anya.

'Very well,' he agreed. And before she could speak again he had gone.

73

7

ANYA was terrified lest she should cry. Blindly she stumbled from the hotel, thankful that James had been called away the moment they reached the main hall.

Monica. . . . The name beat in her brain, the vision re-remained like some menacing ghost to threaten everything upon which her future was to be built. Bitterness, cynicism, withered before the pain of her own hurt. Guy's wife. Nothing said, or even done, could alter that. What did he feel? What did he think as he looked at her, seeing her again after the lapse of years? She was, Anya knew, more attractive than she had envisaged. That pale, fair beauty, doll-like and helpless, was, in its way, as dangerous as the glamour of a sophisticate since it played upon masculine conceit. Her own body felt that it had shrunk a little, that her heart was clutched between pincers that seared and lacerated. A great sickness washed over her in waves. She wasn't conscious of where she was walking, where she was going—anywhere to escape. . . .Would *she* go back to the farm? And why should she be there at all unless she wanted a reconciliation?

Weakly Anya managed to get to an old rustic seat near the end of the drive. She sat down and stared ahead, helplessly struggling against her own vulnerability and realizing the depth and the desperation of her own love.

And suddenly she heard Guy's voice calling her name and almost immediately saw his tall figure rounding the bend of the pathway and coming towards her. She managed not to rush to him, to beat down the agonizing desire to feel his arms about her so that she might tell him of the anguish, the terror within her.

'Darling,' he said, and his voice was low and full of wretchedness, 'I was afraid I might miss you.' His gaze met and held hers. 'I would have done anything to spare you that.'

Anya tried to control her emotions, to cling to a fast crumbling pride. It was not for her to comment. . . . Monica was his wife and as such, in any circumstances, had all the rights. She remained silent, waiting in an agony of suspense to know his reactions, and as though incapable of uttering empty words, he reached out and drew her into his arms, holding her with a suffocating closeness, a tenderness, pressing her face again his shoulder and cupping the back of her head with his hand. Tears stung her eyes and dropped unheeded. She clung to him in desperation, finally gasping: 'Oh, Guy.' And the break in her voice tortured him.

'What does she want?' he demanded. 'Why is she here?'

Anya sat back from him, her eyes searching his face appealingly. 'Haven't you any idea?'

'I?' He shook his head. 'None.' A grim expression hardened his face. 'Unless, in some way Sylvia is at the bottom of it all.'

'But—how?' Anya's heart was thudding so heavily that it made her feel ill. Neither realized that each was asking unanswerable questions, blindly seeking reassurance where there could be none.

Guy's sigh was heavy.

'I'm completely in the dark. It's the very *last* thing. I never thought she'd come back *here*.'

'You mean to this district rather than to England?'

'Yes.' He puckered his brows and then suddenly his attitude changed. 'That's it,' he murmured half to himself. 'Of *course*——'

'What?' Anya hung on every word as he exclaimed:

75

'Divorce—she wants *her* freedom. . . . There can be no other explanation.'

'But couldn't she have communicated with you?' Anya stopped. 'You mean she wants to divorce *you*?'

'Isn't it a reasonable assumption? She said after you and Jimmy left that she wanted to talk to me. . . . And she was the one who wanted to talk—certainly not I.' A worried look came into his eyes. 'What then? To get my freedom I'd have to give her evidence.'

'But *she* deserted *you*?'

'I know, darling, but she could use it as a threat.'

Anya was baffled and struggling to follow the trend of his argument.

'How?'

'By countering any action I might bring for desertion by expressing a willingness to return to me. Until the three years are up. . . . But the more I think of it the more certain I am right about the whole thing.'

Anya saw the viewpoint, but resented the idea that he should be penalized for Monica's former neglect.

'Would you be ready to do as she asked?'

They looked at each other in breathless silence, aware of the possibilities and of every detail of the situation.

'I would do anything that meant making you my wife,' he said quietly.

Anya put out her hand and clasped his. 'And I would do anything that enabled you to be my husband,' she promised significantly.

There was a second of tense, almost electric silence.

'You mean . . .' His gaze burned deeply into hers.

'I mean that if you are to be the guilty person in order to obtain your freedom I want to be associated with you. If we haven't that moral courage in the circumstances, our love for each other wouldn't be very great.'

'But I'd still hate it for you, my darling, and I'd fight every bit of the way to avoid it.'

76

She leaned against him, comforted, secure.

'I love you,' she whispered, as though those three words were the only ones necessary.

His kiss was long, yet curiously gentle, conveying all the depth and power of the emotion surging within him.

'When,' she asked uncertainly, 'are you—you seeing her?'

'At eleven at Green Meadows.'

Anya sat back rather stiffly almost as if finding the situation more than she could bear. His *wife*. . . . She had been real enough before when confined to a distant past. . . . Now she was *there*, in the present, dominating every facet of their lives.

'Not very long to wait,' she said thinly.

'I'll come over the moment I can afterwards,' he promised. 'How long has she booked in at the hotel?'

Anya told him.

He nodded, thinking how in such a brief while everything in his world had changed. Depression returned. He fought it with a fierce and increasing resentment. He would not be victimized by tricks or threats. His gaze travelled over Anya's pale and—despite her attempt at bravery—troubled face and a pang shot through him as he condemned himself for having betrayed his love for her. He had sworn that he would wait until he was free. . . .

'I ought never to have dragged you into all this,' he cried angrily. 'I've no excuse—except loving you too much. And that's a pretty weak confession.'

'A glorious confession,' she insisted, thrilled by the words.

He studied her reflectively and with lingering tenderness.

'And now, my darling, how about my taking you out?' He hastened: 'Don't tell me that I must go home because I've no intention of doing so—I warn you.'

She laughed. 'That rather settles the matter.'

He got to his feet and almost lifted her from the seat.

77

For a second they stood, shoulders touching, and in the deep silence there was harmony and understanding.

.   .   .   .   .

Monica arrived at Green Meadows exactly at eleven o'clock the following morning. Guy, looking at her, realized that she was obviously under a great strain. Her face was pale and her eyes dark-rimmed as though she needed sleep. Her light-weight tweed suit in a rather cold shade of blue was far less kind to her than her gown of the previous night. As she gazed around the once familiar room she realized how little of it she remembered and how attractive it actually looked.

Guy offered her a cigarette which she took. He lit it and his own and said with a distant politeness: 'Very well, Monica, you wanted to talk to me. I'm listening.'

'That sounds terribly formal.'

'Is there any reason why we should be anything other than formal?' He remained standing some way from her and his gaze was steady and distinterested.

She smoothed a hand over the back of her hair. 'I suppose not. You—you hate me for the way I behaved.'

'I am indifferent, Monica.' His voice was smooth and controlled although every nerve in his body was tingling. Just what did she want of him? There was something in her manner that made him both suspicious and afraid. Her helpless, appealing air was not new to him. The thought of Anya was visual, his love and his need of her beyond describing.

'That is worse,' she said pathetically, catching her breath.

'Possibly.' He glanced at his watch. 'If you could tell me how I can help you—or if I can help you—I'd appreciate it. I haven't a great deal of time.'

'I see.'

Again he tried to fathom her mood and failed and irritability flared from suspense.

'Look here,' he said sharply, 'if you won't come to the point, I see no reason for pursuing this meeting. After two and a half years I can hardly be expected to be particularly interested in your moods. But I can assure you——'

'Don't, Guy,' she whispered painfully, and something in her voice froze all further vituperation.

Guy shrank from any evidence calculated to involve him in conflict and rushed in with: 'I think I can tell you exactly what you have in mind.'

She glanced up at him, her manner changing miraculously.

'You—can?' There was eagerness and relief in her voice.

'You want your freedom. That's it, isn't it? But on your own terms. To divorce *me* in fact.'

He never forgot her answer, or the chill that crept over his body as she replied: 'That is the very last thing. I want to—to come *home*, Guy.'

'Home?' He played for time, struggling against the obvious implication of her words. 'But—but you can't mean . . . '

'That is just what I mean—I want your forgiveness for behaving so vilely to you; for walking out. I want another chance.' She added pathetically: 'Everyone has that.'

He stood there stunned, the floor seeming no longer solid beneath his feet, but quicksand into which he could only sink more deeply.

'But,' he gasped, 'why? In heaven's name, Monica——'

Colour crept up into her cheeks, but her gaze was level and held his in a pleading sincerity.

'Because I love you,' she said simply, 'because for two and a half years I've tried to forget you without succeeding, and because loving you I'm home-sick—ill with it.'

Guy felt outraged as he rapped out: 'Do you seriously expect me to believe that for one second? Why, it's fantastic—preposterous. You never loved me and you don't love me now.'

79

She didn't speak for a moment, just sat there unnervingly still, then: 'The first accusation is true, but not the second. And can you think of any possible reason why I should pretend to you? What have I to gain?'

Guy was struggling to counteract the sudden horror that possessed him. The idea that Monica might ever return had been as remote a possibility as that he should invite her to do so. Distrust, fear and depression piled one upon the other as he said: 'The prevention of any divorce action being brought against you for desertion.'

'And why should I worry about that? Surely you can see that unless I were in love with you, the divorce case wouldn't mean a thing to me. I don't need to be kept—alimony in any shape or form. In such circumstances I'd hardly know anything about such an action. What's more I should welcome it since it would leave me free to marry again if I wished.' She added with quiet emphasis: 'I most certainly shouldn't have flown the Atlantic to prevent your divorcing me. . . . In any case I'd no idea you intended doing so.'

Guy didn't want to fall into any trap by betraying his own hand prematurely. Despite his own feelings and desires an instinctive distrust remained.

'Those are you words, not mine,' he exclaimed guardedly.

'Very well. . . .' She sighed. 'I don't mind rejection, but to be denied all credit for sincerity . . . That's different. If you look back, Guy, pretence wasn't really a vice of mine.'

He rushed in with: 'And of course you didn't pretend when you married me?'

'I admitted that wrong; but I didn't perpetuate it—to my sorrow. I shouldn't need to be here now had I done so.'

Emotion almost choked him as he tried to pierce her armour, to find some light in what had suddenly become insufferable darkness.

'Why choose now?' he demanded. 'You must realize how suspicious all this seems.'

'If you believe that, of what use my talking?' she answered patiently.

He stared at her, aware of the light in her eyes as they met his, making him shudder as the tormenting thought took shape; she was his wife . . . his *wife* . . . asking to be taken back, asking for a second chance and all he yearned for was to be able to discredit her without a guilty conscience. He drew a hand across his forehead in a frantic, desperate gesture: 'But it's all absurd . . . we've not seen each other . . .' He stopped because platitudes offended him.

'It's taken me a year to summon up sufficient courage to come here at all.' She looked down at her hands and then lifted her gaze back to his. 'It was being ill that brought all this about.'

'Ill?' It struck him that she was thinner, frailer.

'Yes. At first there was some doubt as to whether or not I'd pull through. But I'm not here to awaken sympathy, only to explain that when one has been apparently near the end, one sees everything so clearly—knows exactly what is important and what is not. I knew then that our marriage was important and that although I had—and I freely admit it— tried to find someone else, to take a lover, it was always of you I thought; always you I wanted. Those are the facts, Guy. I can't change them because you don't want to hear them. . . .'

'It isn't only *that*. . . .' His voice was hoarse.

'And if you want to divorce me you still can, you know.'

'Meaning just what?'

'That I either stay here or—or I shall return to Canada immediately. In which case you are free to bring an action for desertion just as though I'd never visited you.' Her gaze was sad and reproachful. 'I know your opinion of me is very poor, Guy, but I've no desire, I assure you, to upset any plans you may have.'

Guy sat down because his legs felt weighted and there was a dull ache in his heart as though he had been struck a

81

physical blow. He was an essentially fair and just man, and in that moment he could not fall back on any glib retort or justify himself because of the past. The word duty insinuated itself inexorably. He said urgently: 'This cannot be resolved in a moment. I must have time to think it over. We're *strangers*, the whole thing seems ludicrous to me. . . . I'm sorry. . . .' Embarrassment betrayed itself as he saw her wince.

'That's all right,' she said softly, 'I didn't hope that you'd be ready to start again just because I ask it.' Her sigh was deep as she looked around the room. 'It's all so peaceful here. If you *knew* how empty it has been without you.'

He struggled to find some flaw in her attitude, to find the ulterior motive behind this astounding appeal. And unable to do so, said stiffly: 'And if I tell you that I can never return the love you profess——'

'Not "profess",' she chided swiftly. 'Give me that, Guy.'

'Very well then. I repeat the question without the word.'

'You loved me once, why should it be impossible for you to recapture that love?' Her gaze was kindly and unnerving.

'I think La Rochefoucauld answered that better than I could ever do, "We never love a second time where we have once ceased to love".'

'Is that why so many married people come together after separation and unhappiness?'

'Quite possibly since, in such cases, the love has not died.'

'You're very hard.'

'I'm very honest, Monica.' He wanted to tell her about Anya and it was not a question of self-preservation which prevented him, or any lack of courage, merely that instinctively at this stage he wanted to protect Anya and not confuse the issue. He told himself that he could not be expected to accept all that Monica had said without doubt or suspicion. That would merely make him a gullible fool. Only one thing was certain—Anya had all the love of which he was capable and would always have it. Monica, on the other hand, would never be more than a duty, a responsibility whatever the outward symbol of their relationship.

'I appreciate that, provided you will give me credit for the same virtue.'

He sat down in his favourite armchair in a gesture of utter weariness, at a loss for words and consumed by misery and depression.

Monica pressed home her point.

'The fact that I am staying at a hotel proves that I've no wish to jeopardize your future plans. So long as I remain there your grounds for desertion are not imperilled. I promise I will never make a nuisance of myself, Guy.'

He could not ignore what seemed to be her absolute sincerity, he could only shrink from it.

'What about your home in Canada? Your life there?...' He spoke breathlessly, hoping that he might perform some miracle to change her attitude.

'I never had a *home* there,' she replied slowly.

'Yet when, in the beginning, I wrote suggesting that we tried to make a new start you rejected the idea almost contemptuously.' He gained confidence as he spoke, telling himself that in the first confusion he had overlooked many points in his own favour.

She remained calm, a calm that suggested effort and the determination not to make a scene, or cause him embarrassment. But her blue eyes were a little dulled, the corners of her mouth drooped, giving her an almost childish expression, making him feel brutal where he wanted to feel angry.

'I am the first to admit that,' she said remorsefully. 'I was so—so mean then, Guy. Despicable. I'd inherited the money and my conceit was sickening. I've no excuse but, as I explained to you just now, the need that had been growing as the time went by, became simply awful when I was ill. . . . They nearly sent for you, but I wouldn't let them do that. It would have seemed like blackmail. I'm ready to risk coming back knowing that you believe you no longer love me, but

83

not to come back because illness stampeded you into taking me back. Nothing good could come out of that. Only resentment.'

It didn't seem possible that it was Monica talking, he argued despairingly. Before she had been a mixture of cloying sentiment and arrogant assertion. Now every word she uttered was apparently tempered with reason and honesty.

'And you are suggesting that you return here to live,' he said, trying to force home the truth of his own statement and finding it foreign and ludicrous.

'Yes. That I return—your wife,' she said deliberately and steadily.

He didn't hesitate.

'In name only.' His meaning was clear.

She lowered her gaze.

'If that is your ultimatum, very well. I would accept those terms.'

'And if I cannot possibly agree to your coming back here, you——'

'I will leave England and not contest any action for desertion,' she said solemnly, and made a little helpless gesture of supplication. 'How else can I possibly make you believe in me?'

As he sat there he knew he would have given her anything within his power could she prove herself false in this, to him, fantastic desire.

'Assuming that I do believe you, that doesn't mean I could agree to a resumption of married life—even if our relationship was on lines I could accept. No, Monica——'

'You mean,' she cried, and her eyes widened in a fear which amounted to panic, 'you mean your answer is—that'—she stumbled, her voice shaken, her expression stricken—'that you won't consider it?'

He took the only way out.

'I will consider it,' he said flatly, 'but I promise nothing, neither do I give you any hope. There are so many sides to all this.'

She stared at him and for a second he wondered if she might ask him if there was anyone else in his life. But she did nothing of the kind and he was relieved, not because he was afraid to tell her the truth, but because that truth might give her a weapon against Anya. To his intense relief she got to her feet as she said, 'Very well . . . will you get in touch with me?'

'Yes.'

'Let us have a time limit. Suspense is such hell.'

He felt no emotion whatsoever towards her, only an empty despair as he realized the magnitude of the problem now facing him. He wanted to reject her, dismiss her suggestion without further reflection, but she had unarmed him, and all the withering scorn, the vituperation, the condemnation would not help him. His decision must be fair—a just appraisal of the situation. But he knew, even as he faced her, that it would be foreign to him to avail himself of her offer about the divorce action should he refuse to take her back. It would savour of cheating, of hypocrisy, and the idea was distasteful.

'A week,' he said firmly, and escaped into the belief that some miracle would happen during that time.

She left him and he stood staring gloomily out across the farm, his mind in turmoil. Turning back into the house, he saw Graves hovering, obviously agitated. It was not difficult to read his thoughts or to know that while he wanted to make inquiries his position forbade it.

Guy looked at him very steadily. 'That was Mrs Latimer. You probably guessed.'

Graves made no attempt at pretence. 'Well, sir, we heard that she was staying at the hotel. . . .' His expression was apprehensive. 'I—I hope there's nothing wrong, sir.'

Guy said dully: 'I just don't know where I am, Graves.'

'A bit of a shock, as you might say?'

'Yes; a bit of a shock.'

'I'm sorry, sir.'

Guy looked at him and said gently: 'Thanks, Graves. I know I can rely on you in every way—particularly when it comes to keeping your own counsel.'

'That indeed you can, sir. And that goes for my wife.'

Guy nodded his appreciation. Now there was only one thing uppermost in his mind—to talk to Anya as soon as it was possible.

8

ANYA met Guy that evening and he drove her back to Green Meadows in order that they could talk without interruption. Alone in his small study-cum-office, he outlined all that had been said by Monica, ending with: 'I still can't believe it has happened. It's rather like a nightmare.'

Anya, despite the heat of the summer evening, was cold to the point of shivering. Every word had beaten into her heart making it hurt and taking every scrap of strength from her body. Monica wanted to return to him. A simple enough statement, but one that splintered every hope and made her life disintegrate. A feeling of nausea went over her as, trying to keep her voice from shaking, she said: 'Isn't it very much a matter of how you feel?'

He echoed her words aghast, then: 'Aren't my feelings obvious?' His gaze met hers.

'Not necessarily, Guy.'

He puckered his brows, the question in his eyes. 'How can I feel except staggered, or perhaps shattered would be a better word.'

'Because you think you ought to—to take her back?' Anya fought against the pain within her; pain that threatened reason and understanding, and made jealousy stab with the sharpness of a knife.

'Duty,' he murmured with distaste. 'I don't know where I am.'

Anya couldn't keep back the words. 'Couldn't that be because you are not sure of your real feelings for her—when it comes to it?'

Guy, manlike, could not appreciate her reactions to the subtler implications of the situation.

'My feelings for her have nothing to do with it. I'm not involved emotionally where she's concerned.'

'Then is there a problem?' She hadn't intended to say that.

'Meaning that I should have refused to listen to her?'

Colour mounted Anya's cheeks. 'Meaning'—she corrected—'that only you can make a decision.'

The conversation had slanted in a direction foreign to his intentions, and contrary to his feelings. All he could think of was the possibility of his future with Anya being threatened and how best to keep her in his life. That she might assume from his attitude that this was not the case never occurred to him.

'I didn't want you dragged into the divorce action,' he said almost fiercely. 'Yet now, knowing she wants to return to me, could I decently, honestly, sue her for desertion—as she *has* agreed that I should do if——'

'If you don't begin married life with her again?'

He nodded, his thoughts rushing ahead as he exclaimed: 'I can't quite grasp what is fair or right. I know only what I want—for *us*.' His gaze held hers as suddenly it struck him that she had become remote and he gasped: 'Anya, for heaven's sake, help me.'

'How can I?' she said quietly.

It was one of those moments in a human relationship when great love—mutual love—was its own enemy and the destructive thought shot through his mind: 'Can she, Anya, after all, care so very much and be so unhelpful, so curiously aloof?' And in her turn Anya asked: 'Would he need my help if he really loved *me*, wouldn't he have refused even to consider taking Monica back?' It went beyond the question of mere right or wrong, and became an elemental struggle, a violent rivalry.

He burst out: 'But you know your reactions to any

divorce action and to my being the guilty party—involving you.'

'So do you know them. I've told you before that I'm prepared to do anything.' She broke off. 'I don't think that angle is the problem. But I certainly appreciate that, in the present circumstances, you could not sue on a false issue. I'd hate that, it would seem mean—like cheating.'

He knew that she was right and nodded gloomily. His arms went out and drew her close to him as he cried: 'I can't lose you, my darling. I won't give you up.'

Anya's lips parted to his as she clung to him and the frenzy of passion brought them momentary oblivion. But even as she drew back, the implication of his words—that he was already considering the possibility that he might have to give her up—stabbed to bring a hollow emptiness to her heart. Her voice was almost emotionless as she said: 'That tells me a very great deal, Guy.' A faint cynicism sharpened her tone as she added: 'I'm afraid you will have to give one of us up.'

And even as she spoke the echo of her mother's words taunted and mocked her. *He will hurt you in the end.*

He stared at her almost as if she had struck him. 'Don't,' he whispered painfully, 'put it like that.'

'We can't avoid the facts,' she persisted.

'We can avoid distorting them.'

Anya struggled to cling to reason, to rationalize the situation and lift it out of its dangerous emotionalism.

'Suppose you tell me exactly how you see all this, Guy. I can't get into your mind, your heart.'

'Doesn't the fact that you know I love you explain this whole business?'

'No.' She was adamant. 'Thousands of men—married men'—she spoke deliberately—'*love* other women until it comes to a crisis. Then love, curiously enough, counts for nothing against a far more overwhelming factor. To deceive myself now would hardly help either of us.'

He cut in sharply. 'I had already made my plans for the future; there was no question of my regard for Monica coming into it.'

'I agree but, then, Monica was thousands of miles away. You didn't make that decision to divorce her while she was in the picture. Now that she has returned you are immediately uncertain.'

'But,' he persisted, 'not because of my feelings for her, the woman.'

'What then?'

'Because of—of duty, the fact that she is my wife.'

'She was your wife yesterday,' Anya went on deliberately.

'But with a very considerable difference,' he cried urgently. 'Then, apparently she was as indifferent to me as I to her. And that indifference on her part—her desertion as well—set me morally free. Now that picture has entirely changed.'

Anya shivered. It was like standing back and watching an avalanche that was bound to destroy her. She said quietly: 'I appreciate all that, Guy.'

'But I want you to *understand* it,' he burst out imploringly, 'and not imagine the wrong thing.' His expression was a little baffled. The scene had not gone as he'd envisaged it, almost as though a blind had been drawn down between them.

'I don't think I'm likely to do that.' Her gaze was very steady. 'It comes to a question of hurt. . . .'

A question of hurt. . . . Guy groaned inwardly. To hurt Anya in order to appease Monica outraged his sense of justice, even discounting the fact that his own destruction would be encompassed in it. . . . The idea of hurting Monica, on the other hand, was not to him a wholly personal issue, but rather a far larger problem involving conscience and responsibility. Monica, the woman, he was no longer concerned with; his love for her—if it had ever been love—was dead; but Monica, his wife, imposed upon him the duties indivisible with marriage. And he could not deceive himself

90

into believing that in different circumstances (while knowing his *wife* loved him and wanted to be with him) he would ever have considered leaving her. The question was how far the morality of that issue devolved upon him at that moment since Monica had deserted him in the beginning. Did that absolve him, justify him in disregarding her plea? Did that automatically set him free? And if it didn't, could he ever find happiness for himself or give it to Anya? Would Monica be the shadow lying between them?

His sigh was deep. He shook his head.

'There is no difference between hurting you, my darling, and hurting myself. The two things are one.'

A little of the tension that had made Anya sick with fear and misery lessened. She had struggled to find out the truth, to tear down any façade he might have built up in order to spare her. Now she yearned to comfort and to give him strength as she said: 'I can't sit in your chair, Guy. I can only imagine how I should feel in your place—which is not the same thing.'

'There's only one thing I can feel,' he said almost violently. 'Despair and anger—yes, anger—because this has happened. Life on Monica's terms. Our hopes, in any case, of all this being settled without unpleasantness, ruined. I can't divorce her now. She knows that,' he finished grimly, frustration whipping him to fury.

His anger released the pent-up misery that had made Anya desolate and she told herself that she had mistaken his innate honesty and fairness to mean lack of love for her. Instantly all the warmth and generosity within her surged out to him and she cried: 'Oh, darling, I do understand, but what can I say?'

His gaze was steady and searching. 'That you love me.' There was no emotion in his voice, only a note of gravity.

She threw herself down on the floor beside his chair as he sat down, her arms curved to rest upon his knees, her hands held his.

91

'I love you too much, perhaps,' she answered solemnly.

'God knows it was never my intention to get you into all this. I'd every justification for believing in the future.' His brows puckered into a worried frown. 'I feel that I'm looking at a picture with one part missing. Monica was so—so pathetic.'

Anya felt the sickness steal back. She could not escape the torturing thought that men were mostly deceived by that very pose. Yet what right had she to judge Monica?

'The idea of *her*'—Guy went on—'admitting she was in the wrong, apologizing and——'

'And—what?' Anya's voice quivered as she tried to curb her emotion.

'Almost pleading,' he said tensely. 'The whole thing—it's fantastic. Why should I consider her after all that has happened? Concern myself with her point of view? She left me of her own free will.' He was like a man arguing with himself, struggling to find some hope, some light in the dark world of tomorrow.

Anya's heart felt that a great weight was crushing it.

'Only you can answer that question,' she said, and there was a stillness about her as she slowly sat back on her heels and looked at him. She never forgot that moment. . . . The warm summer evening, the sunlight filtering through the deep windows; the patchwork of the farm lands spread like a carpet that was lost in the sky, and in the silent room, the grandfather clock ticking, every second holding her destiny.

She asked a final question. 'What did you say to her?'

'Very little.' As he sat there his confusion and misery was so great that actual words eluded him. In any case it didn't seem to matter. 'I told her I would give her my answer in a week. A week,' he added bitterly.

Anya turned away because the tears were stinging her eyes and she was afraid of his seeing them.

'That will at least give you time to make your decision,' she said hollowly.

92

He leaned forward, his expression fearful: 'That sounded so—so detached, darling.'

She got to her feet. 'It is all that is allowed me, Guy. To influence you in any way would be wrong.'

'But,' he cried, 'it isn't a question of that. I can't think beyond us and all that is involved for us.' He had moved from his chair to stand beside her. 'To hurt *you*——' As he spoke he was thinking of divorce action and of the method by which he would now have to obtain his freedom should he reject Monica's plea.

Anya, womanlike, caught at that as evidence of his intention to take Monica back. It seemed tantamount to an admission that he would not consider a divorce.

'Suppose we don't talk of it any more, Guy.' Her voice broke.

He clutched at that, desolate in his conflict. How, he argued, could he be sure that Monica was sincere? Why should he credit her with any nobility of purpose? Suppose she had some ulterior motive. . . . Her insistence that if his verdict went against her she would not contest any action he brought against her, but would return quietly to Canada . . . was there some trick in that too? He looked down at Anya and his heart seemed wrenched out of position at the idea of dragging her into some sordid fight in which he would offer little protection from public gossip. Divorce, in itself, was nothing, he knew, but without trust in Monica's good intentions, Anya's name might well become cheapened, and the whole thing turned into a sensational affair. That being so, wasn't it his duty to take Monica back. . . . If only to protect Anya from her. As against that, what ulterior motive *could* Monica have? What had she to gain, even as she had pointed out.

'It isn't possible,' he said grimly, 'to trust once you have known a person capable of bad faith.'

'And you want to believe in her,' Anya said chokingly.

'I want to be quite sure what I am fighting.' He added and

his voice was hoarse with an emotion greater than any she had ever heard him betray before. 'I've got to protect you, my darling, quite apart from this whole wretched business.'

A new light came into Anya's eyes, new hope to her heart.

'Does—does she know about me—us?'

'No,' he said with some vehemence, 'I was not going to give her any weapons. Even if I would consider taking her back, I'd want to be very much more sure of her sincerity than I am now.' He brightened. 'It's so easy to give a person credit for the truth; so easy when you're listening to them saying all the right things, giving all the right answers at a time when you're too distracted even to know the questions —that's when you are most gullible. . . .' As he spoke he put his arms around Anya's shoulders, kissing her forehead, her eyes, her lips with a gentleness that tore at her control. 'I love you,' he whispered. 'Anya, I love you.'

Her body trembled against his, his words were balm to her anguished mind.

'Then nothing else matters,' she cried. 'Nothing.' There was frenzy in the utterance—a frenzy matching his own. And in the passion of that moment fear vanished.

Guy drove her back to the pathway leading to the hotel grounds, avoiding the main entrance.

'This is what I detest,' he said grimly, 'leaving you.' His gaze held hers. 'Oh, Anya, have I any earthly right to make a decision which is going to drag you into the divorce court? It wasn't my idea of our relationship. . . .'

Her voice was firm and strong as she answered him. 'My being drawn into any action is of no consequence—none. Remember that. The real issue is between yourself and—and Monica.' She could not bring herself to utter the word wife. 'If you feel that your future lies with her——'

'It wouldn't be my future,' he cried fiercely. 'You must understand that. My future is with you. But unfortunately my love for you doesn't automatically make me a free man as I believed I should be. That being so——' He stopped and added gently: 'I'd like to get all this settled, my darling, before I see you again. This is torture for us both.'

Anya asked herself just how she was going to live through the suspense of the days ahead. She felt ill and almost desperate as she looked at him. Suppose this were to be the end of all her dreams? Somehow she managed to say: 'Of course . . . it's better that way.'

He made a little gesture of helplessness.

'Even now I can't believe it,' he exclaimed wretchedly.

'I must go.' She spoke in a whisper, her voice breathless, misery washing over her as despair took the place of what had once been happiness.

'I'll ring you,' he promised.

'Very well.'

Stilted words that echoed her acceptance and hid the hunger within her. She wanted to throw herself into his arms, to implore him not to leave her. There was panic in her eyes which the kindly darkness hid from him.

He bent swiftly and kissed her, feeling her soft warm lips part in passionate desire, her body grow taut against his, her arms encircle his neck almost as though this were a last embrace.

'Darling,' he murmured softly.

For an instant her eyes met his gaze as the moon poured its radiance upon her face and then, swiftly, like a pale ghost, she turned away and began to run from him and although he called her name she neither stopped nor looked back. Sobs tore at her, tears ran down her cheeks. She heard his car engine racing, drive away as though that, too, was aware of the urgency, the desperation that made speed almost a necessity, an expression of a fundamental need for escape.

Gasping, almost reeling with exhaustion, Anya reached a giant elm tree and clutched at it for support seeing, to her consternation, James coming towards her, quickening his pace as he realized her distress.

95

'Why, Anya! My dear girl, what is it? You look like death.'

Anya didn't pretend.

'I feel like it.'

'Want to talk about it?' He lit a cigarette and handed it to her, then lit another for himself. 'Come over here to that tree stump, you'll be better sitting down.' He supported her as she moved the short distance.

'Thank you. . . . Sorry.'

He flicked out a handkerchief. 'Your eye stuff's smudged,' he said laconically.

She managed to control her emotions, to take a deep breath and stop crying. 'I must look hideous.'

'Just unhappy,' he said in his lilting voice. 'That damned woman turning up just when everything was going smoothly.

Anya started and lowered the mirror which she had taken from her handbag, and was holding so that she could repair her make-up.

'Woman?' She tried to sound innocent.

'Monica. . . . You don't think you've fooled me—do you?'

'I didn't want to fool you.'

'I'll accept that. . . . Blast her—just when Guy was beginning to find life worth living.'

Anya felt the old anguish steal back. 'Meaning that he hadn't done so since she left?'

James snorted. 'And if that's not just like a woman! Jumping to conclusions, hurling herself over the precipice before she's even made sure she's any reason for committing suicide. 'No, I meant—you.'

'Oh.' She sighed, calmer for the outlet of tears. 'I'd like your opinion, James.'

'It's yours for what it's worth, my dear girl.'

Her eyes met his, the moonlight turning night almost into day. Suddenly she knew that they were no longer employer and employee, but friends.

96

'Then if there should be any possibility of a reconciliation between Guy and his wife . . . Ought I to make things easy ——' She broke off, the anguish within her almost unbearable.

'By getting out of the picture?'

'Yes.'

'That's a pretty leading question. I never believe in noble sacrifices unless they're in a good cause, and I'd need a heck of a lot of convincing that Monica could ever be that. Guy's another matter.' He looked at her unflinchingly as he added: 'On the other hand marriage itself presents its own problem and has its priority. Was that what you meant?'

'I suppose it was.' Away from Guy she could think more clearly, allow the truth to sink in divorced from emotionalism.

'But why should there be any question of a reconciliation?'

Anya answered guardedly, 'I was speaking hypothetically.'

'That won't get us very far.'

'I'd still like your opinion in the event of it no longer being hypothetical. You know Guy very well. You were best man at—at his wedding,' she finished shakenly.

'Then I'd say this to you: whatever Guy did he would have to be at peace with himself. Not because he'd claim any special virtues, but because he'd loathe to be unfair or unjust.'

Anya nodded.

'And if there are decisions to be made he's more than capable of making them. When the question at stake is the future of a marriage only the two people concerned can be the final judges. Marriage is a damned queer relationship and I'm far too canny to hazard any guesses about the behaviour of those within it. Afraid I've not been much help.' His gaze was steady and sympathetic. 'But don't go rushing in the wrong direction believing you are doing the right thing.'

'I know what you mean.' A faint smile touched her lips. 'The precipice?'

'Exactly.'

'Thank you, James.'

'I'm quite sure you don't feel any better, my dear, but I'd like you to know I understand.'

'Does Guy realize that?'

'Undoubtedly. We've never needed words he and I.' His brows puckered. 'But I will allow myself one observation, that I can't for the life of me fathom just why Monica has suddenly decided to come back here. What's more I'm damned sorry she has.' He paused, then: 'On the other hand I must say that she seems to have changed considerably.'

'How?' Anya's mouth felt dry as she fought against the misery and depression engulfing her.

'Gentler; less contradictory . . . pathetic, somehow.'

Pathetic . . . Guy's word, Anya thought desperately.

They began to walk back to the hotel. The hollow emptiness clawed at Anya as though her body were a vacuum. The night became a tapestry on which was painted the dark phantoms of fear, the heartache of loving. As they reached the main hall Monica, to Anya's dismay, came towards them.

'Hello,' she said with a quiet friendliness. Her keen woman's eye took note of Anya's pale face, her haunted eyes, and in a low sympathetic voice she murmured: 'Miss Rutherford, are you all right?'

James came to the rescue. 'Miss Rutherford has a vile head —not the convenient excuse variety.'

Anya blessed him.

'A hateful admission,' she managed to say, 'but if you'll forgive me I'm going early to bed.'

'Of course.' Monica smiled. 'I hope you'll feel better in the morning.'

'Thank you.'

Anya escaped, feeling that she had suddenly been projected into some world of fantasy in which not even she were real. She tried to be objective about the situation, to cling to the knowledge of Guy's love for her. But her heart ached and nothing she could tell herself consoled her. Only her mother's words echoed in the deathly silence of the room which had suddenly become a prison. Her mind swung from one tormenting thought to another. Nothing could alter the fact that Monica was Guy's wife and that marriage gave her all the advantages of an insurance policy on which she paid no premium. Was it possible that a woman—who had left her husband the moment she inherited money—could ever have loved him, or that being away from him for two and a half years she could suddenly return, genuinely anxious to begin life with him again?

Anya's body felt as if it was stretched on an invisible rack, every nerve tingled. There was nothing she could say, or do. It was not for her to plead her own cause. She had no rights, no justification for seeking to undermine any loyalty Guy might feel. And she wouldn't have him other than just and fair even as James had said. In a few days the situation would resolve itself. . . . A few days. . . .

She tried to sleep, to escape from the conflict and the conjecture, but when the night had passed and it was time to get up she had not closed her eyes. . . .

9

UNA COLBY took one look at Anya that morning and said: 'Good heavens, you look ghastly.'

Anya tried to laugh. Somehow she must get through the day; somehow she must find some trivial excuse for her pallor which her rouge could not conceal, but merely emphasize.

'I feel it. Something I ate, I suppose. . . . Haven't slept all night.'

James hurried into the office at that moment, glancing at Anya with concern. 'I hope your head is better.'

Una Colby looked surprised. So it was a physical ill. She'd decided that there was some link between Anya and Guy Latimer which the appearance of his wife under her maiden name—a fact which had gone around the hotel like a news flash—complicated. Evidently her imagination had run riot, Una Colby concluded.

'I'm afraid not. Work will help it to wear off. . . . I've the confirmation of the Sir Gerald booking, by the way.'

'Good. . . . You go in and get something to eat,' he insisted. 'And some strong coffee.'

Anya hastily refused. She had just seen Monica go into the dining-room.

'Then I'll have it sent to you here and you'll drink it, young lady. Orders.'

Anya thanked him, trying to concentrate upon her job, working automatically and wondering if Guy would telephone her. How ridiculous, that would be the last thing

just now. Indiscreet. She ached to hear his voice, to be re-
assured of his love for her, and then told herself in disgust
that she was weak and flabby where she should be strong
and resourceful while knowing that suspense was the worst
thing she could be asked to bear. At that moment the telephone rang and while she had dozens of calls a day, her
heart missed a beat and when the switchboard operator said:
'Miss Rutherford, I've a personal call for you, would you
like to take it in the box,' she gasped, colour rising to her
pale cheeks.

'Please . . . yes. . . .' For a second the world was a bubble
of light as she ran across the wide hall into the kiosk nearby, picking up the receiver, her voice eager, then: '*Daphne!*'

She recovered swiftly as Daphne said: 'Don't sound so
disappointed. Sorry I'm not Guy. . . . But I simply had to
tell you. . . . Paul's wife's divorcing him. . . . It's all settled.
We're going to be married as soon as he's free. Oh, Anya, I'm
so happy. . . . And I knew you'd be glad for me.' Her
laughter was lilting. 'Stop your worrying about me, too. . . .
We're coming down to Wyvern this week-end. Paul wants
to talk to Daddy and not be thought quite a cad. As if I
cared, so long as we can be together! I say . . . are you all
right? Oh, damn the pips. No more change. . . . Good-bye,
see you at the week-end. I'll ring you. 'Bye.'

Anya replaced the receiver and went back to her desk.
The happiness in Daphne's voice contrasted sharply with
her own misery, but she was thankful that at least Paul had
proved his sincerity. . . . She hated the dark suspicion that
lingered in her mind lest Guy might not; lest his love for
her had been only the diversion because Monica had left
him. . . . A shudder went over her. The thought was horrible
and sordid and she blamed herself for it, without being able
to escape its implications.

She heard from Guy two days later, seeing his handwriting almost with dread superimposed upon the initial
happiness. He wrote:

My darling,

    I've to go up to London for a couple of days in connection with rather dreary farm business, and hope to be back on Friday afternoon. Would you ring me about five o'clock so that we can have dinner together?

    Forgive this miserable rushed note, but I must catch the post. I long to see and to talk to you.

Guy

Her hands shook as she put the sheet of writing paper back into its envelope. *I long to see and to talk to you. . . .* Friday. . . . Her hopes soared; the suspense diminished. At least the initiative was with her since she could ring him.

'Someone given you a fortune,' Una Colby said, conscious of Anya's altered expression as she started work.

'Perhaps! It depends on what you mean by fortune. But it's a lovely day and my day off.'

'Going home?'

'Yes. I haven't seen my father for a fortnight.'

Una chuckled. 'But your father hasn't brought that sparkle to your eyes, my dear!'

Anya smiled without confusion. 'No.'

'We've had the deep depression over Iceland since Monday. Glad the trough of high pressure has caught up again.' She stopped abruptly as Monica paused at the reception-desk.

'I'm glad to see you are looking better, Miss Rutherford,' she said quietly, and her expression was full of solicitude.

'Thank you,' Anya managed to say, noticing Monica's well-tailored coffee-coloured suit with all the matching accessories. Everything she wore was expensive and she managed to convey a delicate fragility which was appealing.

'I'm going up to London for the day and may stay overnight—perhaps until Friday. It rather depends on our plans.' She handed in her key as she spoke and then smiled apologetically. 'I'm sorry, I should give that to the porters, shouldn't I?'

Anya could not keep back the suspicion that darted into her mind like some deadly poison. . . . London. . . . *Our plans*. . . . Was it possible that she was meeting Guy? That the business trip was, in truth, one with *her*? Anya struggled to sound casual and pleasant as she murmured: 'That's quite all right. I'll attend to it.'

'And would you be kind enough to tell Jimmy—Mr Fawcett? I was to have had luncheon with him today.'

Anya managed to smile her assent. Then: 'Here is Mr Fawcett,' she said, as James came in from the garden entrance.

Monica beamed at him, and remained at the reception-desk as she exclaimed: 'Jimmy, I'd just given Miss Rutherford a message for you. . . . I've an appointment in London . . . a luncheon date. . . . I know you'll forgive me. I must fly. . . . Train? Yes. I'm meeting Guy. . . . We thought it might be a good idea to go back to one or two of our old haunts. There's so much to discuss and to plan. . . .' She had lowered her voice to a confidential tone, but it carried to Anya's ears as though shouted through a loudspeaker, making her feel that every drop of blood in her body was icy and that her heart was about to stop beating. Not being able to endure more she managed to move out of earshot and finally to reach her own room.

There she stood, her back against the door, hardly able to move because of the sickness washing over her, the dread suspicions mounting in her already tormented mind. Guy's letter, his words '*I've to go up to London for a couple of days in connection with rather dreary farm business*. . . . And all the time he was to meet Monica. That being so, why—*why* couldn't he have been honest? She gave a little groan and stumbled to the edge of the bed, flopping down upon it, fighting the sobs tearing at her. On reflection, wasn't that a very stilted little note from a man supposedly in love? *I long*

103

to see and to talk to you. . . . She had hugged those words, reading into them a wealth of meaning, refusing to allow anything to rob her of the balm of them, but now, even they were suspect.

She took a deep breath; somehow she must calm herself; somehow she must go back to work. It was so easy to jump to the wrong conclusions. Her mood changed. Because Guy was seeing Monica didn't automatically mean their reconcil-iation. . . . Perhaps he didn't want to worry her, Anya, by mentioning his plans in a note—a hurried note at that. Why think of all the things most calculated to hurt her? On Friday she would see Guy and know the truth. Until then if she loved him she must trust him. It was hardly likely that he would come to any decision without discussing the future again with Monica. *'We thought it a good idea to go back to one or two of our old haunts.'* Weren't those words full of significance, implying a mutuality of purpose? She pressed her hands against her cheeks, closing her eyes, fighting to calm herself. It appalled her because of the anguish that re-duced her to such a state of weakness. It was foreign to her own conception of character; foreign to everything she admired. *Love!* For a second she allowed cynicism to pour a veneer over the deep hurt within her. Whatever happened, she'd only herself to blame for the circumstances. She got to her feet, powdered her face and returned to work. Monica had left and she was grateful for the fact that she didn't see James again that morning.

Graham called for her after luncheon that afternoon. She had telephoned him in answer to his request and was even grateful for his company and the suggestion that he should drive her over to Wyvern. He eyed her with keen, almost critical gaze.

'I can't say that working has improved your health. You don't look at all well.'

She was too dispirited to argue.

'Tension. I'm beginning to settle in though.' As she sat

in the car she recalled a conversation she'd had with him about Guy and marriage in general soon after her mother's death. How insistent he'd been that the fact of Monica having been away affected the whole situation.

'It wouldn't have anything to do with the return of Monica Latimer by any chance?'

'How did you know she was back?'

Graham laughed scornfully. 'My dear girl, don't be ridiculous. Her friend Sylvia March is a day ahead of any newspaper.'

'You know Mrs March?' Anya tried to sound casual.

'Yes; we're acting for her in a professional matter. She seems to think that Mrs Latimer is staying in England.'

'Really.' Anya's lips felt stiff, her throat muscles paralysed.

'And that she will return to Green Meadows.' Graham's own hurt found an outlet in the belief that he was causing Anya uneasiness.

'Time,' Anya managed to retort, 'will prove whether or not that is true.'

'Don't *you* know?'

'Why should I?'

'I thought Latimer was such a great friend.' Graham hated himself because of his own jealousy that fed on the fear lest Anya should really be in love with Guy.

'Then I can assure you I haven't any idea whether or not Guy Latimer'—she managed to keep her voice quiet and cool—'and his—his wife will be reconciled. That is their affair.'

'I'd be much happier,' Graham said with sudden gentleness, 'if I could be sure that it wasn't your affair also.'

'And did Mrs March enlighten you on that point?'

Graham shot her a swift glance. 'Why should she?'

'I just wondered. I met her once—just for a few seconds. The gossipy type.'

'I don't agree. I found her charming and most concerned for Monica Latimer.'

105

'So the subject was mentioned.'

'Yes.'

'And she no doubt told you how devoted Guy was to his wife.'

'No; how deeply in love she was with *him*.'

'Was that why she had lived apart from him all this time?' Anya said, trying not to explode.

Graham struck the last blow. 'That doesn't alter the fact that she is still his wife and is fully entitled to return to him if she wishes. And, of course, if *he* wishes.' He finished sharply: 'It isn't a crime to rectify a mistake, you know. You may remember that I warned you about the strange ties of marriage and how cut up he was when she left him.'

Anya knew that she must not satisfy his curiosity regarding her own involvement, but his words were knives cutting into her heart.

'I remember, although as for the warning . . . Do we have to discuss Mr Latimer every time we meet?'

'Yes,' he said, his control snapping. 'I think I could bear it if only I knew what the situation was between you two.'

'Oh, Graham,' she cried, 'please don't begin again. . . .'

'I don't want you to get mixed up in any of it,' he persisted. 'And if you're in love with each other why the devil can't you come out in the open and say so?'

'If and when that fact is ever established,' she replied forcefully, 'we will.'

'And just what am I supposed to make of that?'

'Just what you want to make of it,' she said wearily.

'That leaves me only one conclusion. That you're at his mercy and unsure of him.'

Anya winced; it was so near the truth.

'Aren't you rather forgetting the little matter of his wife?'

'Aren't *you*?' he snapped.

Anya's voice was suddenly authoritative. 'Either we change this conversation, or stop the car and let me get out.

106

I value your friendship, Graham, but I'm not on the witness stand.'

He was instantly contrite. 'I vowed to myself I wouldn't mention the damned business,' he cried apologetically, 'but I've only to see you and think of him and I want to commit murder. You're unhappy. I'm not quite blind. And —and—there's nothing I can do except watch you suffering. I love you,' he added vehemently and almost aggressively.

Anya softened. 'I understand Graham. And I do appreciate your point of view.'

He slowed the car down. 'Would you marry me, let me take care of you if—if things should go wrong?'

His words hung significantly between them and she had no challenge left to counteract them.

'Would you really want me to do so in such circumstances?'

'Yes.' He spoke belligerently. 'I'd make you forget because he wouldn't be worth a damn if he let you down. I'm all for any man being loyal to his wife, but what infuriates me is the one who involves another poor deluded woman in his wretched affairs when, in his heart, he's still involved with his wife. It's amazing, too, how when it suits him he can hide behind duty, and all the rest of it, to excuse his fickleness.'

A shudder went over Anya, but she refused to associate the words with her own affairs. Her voice was firm. 'No two sets of circumstances are alike and there is so simple answer —or common judgement—for these cases. One can know ninety per cent of any story, but it is the unknown five per cent that puts it all in perspective.'

'Would you argue like that if you were the woman let down?' He wanted to wrest the truth from her.

'Not having been let down I cannot say.'

'But just now you more or less admitted that——'

'I admitted nothing, Graham. We were both being hypothetical.

'By heaven,' he cried, 'you're loyal.'

'That makes two of us,' she said, and her inflection silenced him.

They drove to Wyvern and her father welcomed her with more warmth than he had ever betrayed in his life before. The house, under the care of Mrs Bradstock, was running perfectly and he was happier than at any time since his unfortunate marriage. He often felt guilty because Harriet's death had released him from his own inhibitions.

'And you like your job?' he inquired with interest.

'Very much.'

'I meant to run over,' he hastened, 'but to be honest I've been going out a bit myself.' His smile was a little shy and he avoided Anya's gaze.

'Anyone I know?' she asked encouragingly.

He gave a nervous laugh. 'No.'

Graham helped him out. 'A glamorous widow, if you but knew it, Anya.'

'Loreli Fairfax,' Marcus ventured tentatively.

Young?' Anya prompted.

'Forty,' he admitted. He was fifty-four.

There was a second of silence which Anya broke with: 'Oh, Daddy, I'm so glad. . . . Please be happy. It's what Daphne and I want most for you.'

'I was pretty obnoxious when you suggested my marrying again,' he said reminiscently. 'I suppose you must have always thought me a crashing bore. Pompous as they make them.'

Was this, Anya asked herself in amazement, her father talking?

'Frankly, at times, yes.'

They laughed together.

'I've learned a great deal lately,' he admitted. 'I suppose it seems ridiculous to you, I mean, in a way . . . The idea of my being——'

'In love,' she said quietly.

108

'Yes.' There was no hesitation in his voice.

'Not in the least, why should it? I wasn't so blind that I didn't appreciate the penalties of your life with Mummie—and that doesn't mean I was indifferent to her suffering. But I certainly didn't regard you as the ideal partners even before her illness. Children aren't idiots, incapable of seeing behind a façade. If anything they loathe that façade—contrary to general belief.'

'I suppose,' he admitted, 'most parents are cowards about that sort of thing. They want to delude themselves that they've given their children a happy home and set a good example.'

'Loreli,' murmured Anya softly. 'A lovely name.'

'She could come over this evening and meet you,' he said eagerly.

When Loreli arrived it seemed hardly possible that she was forty, for she had the clear skin, the starry eyes of a young girl and while her clothes were glamorous, everything about her smart and elegant, she managed to convey a warmth and enthusiasm which made her loved by most people with whom she came in contact.

Watching her, Anya felt a pang, a crushing loneliness. If only Guy might be with her. Instead, he was most likely with Monica . . . *'one of our old haunts.'* She could hardly bear the thought.

'It's wonderful to meet you,' Loreli said, and sighed her relief. She looked lovingly at Marcus. 'Although how he could ever have worried lest you wouldn't understand our—out friendship is beyond me.'

'My worry,' Anya said with a broad smile, 'is that you don't waste time on friendship. Every hour is important. You *are* going to be married—aren't you?'

Marcus gazed at Loreli. 'Are we?' he whispered.

She went close to him. 'I must say I hoped I'd be asked!'

Anya gasped. 'Well! If that isn't a proposal worthy of my father, I don't know. *Daddy!*'

After that, they settled down to an evening such as Wyvern had never seen before. Just before leaving Anya had an opportunity of talking to Loreli alone, studying her calm, serene beauty which nevertheless held a radiance which prevented it being cold or remote. There was a quality about her which Anya knew would bring harmony to her father's hitherto discordant life and she said gently: 'You'll never know how grateful I am to you . . . you've transformed Daddy—made him a human being. He wasn't one before.'

'I know. That's what he told me. I can understand, too.'

'You?' Anya's surprise was obvious.

'I was not happy before. . . . There was such an emptiness. It isn't a question of who was right or who wrong, just a matter of temperaments, I suppose. Or the depth of one's feelings. With Marcus, everything is fun. I'm alive . . . and now to know that we can be friends, Anya.'

Anya bent and kissed her cheek. 'Bless you.' Her voice was low.

'And—Daphne?'

'She'll be just as glad as I. In any case, she has some news which I mustn't disclose for her. . . .'

'And you—your life?' Loreli looked at Anya steadily, aware of the haunting sadness behind the brave smile and of the shadow of fear lurking in her eyes.

'Complicated at the moment.' Anya sensed understanding in the murmur Loreli gave, in which there was solicitude without curiosity.

'I married originally to escape from a complication,' Loreli admitted honestly. 'If ever you want to talk to anyone who can forget that a confidence has been made . . . I'm here.'

In that moment there was a strange wisdom in Loreli's expression and where, to begin with, Anya had felt years older than she, now, she realized that here was a woman who could be strong and resolute, a bulwark against trouble.

'I won't forget that,' she promised.

Marcus called to them from an adjoining room.

'We're coming,' Anya called back, and laughed at his impatience. 'In any case I must be going.'

'Graham will run you back?' Loreli inquired.

'Yes.'

'He's been awfully sweet.'

'Graham's a wonderful friend,' Anya said quietly.

Loreli didn't speak, but there was a strange sympathy in her silence.

At the second of leaving the house, Anya said to her father: 'I'll expect you to have the wedding date fixed by the time I come over at the week-end.' She glanced from his beaming countenance to Loreli's.

'We'll have it fixed,' he said stoutly, and surreptitiously clasped Loreli's hand. 'Daphne wrote that she's coming down and bringing a friend with her. Some new attraction, I expect.'

Anya said nothing, but hurried Graham away from the front door. She was afraid lest he might know about Paul and, given a lead, divulge facts which Daphne preferred to explain herself.

In the car on the homeward journey, Graham said: 'Well, now you know! I've watched that little romance for weeks. Glad?'

'Delighted.'

'Your father's a different person. . . .'

Anya thought of her mother with sadness. There had been so much misery for her, so little compensation, but even had she been strong and healthy she could never have brought that particular look to her husband's eyes—a look which Loreli had miraculously achieved. There was either love or there was not . . . and without it—emptiness, frustration. And a final bitterness.

'How little we know about each other,' she mused. 'Half the time we see people giving the impersonations we expect of them.'

'Such as yours tonight,' Graham said startlingly.

Anya was instantly defensive.

'Impersonation! I was utterly sincere about them; enormously glad, thankful even. Selfish, too. It will be wonderful to have a real home to visit from time to time—a happy home.'

'Sorry,' Graham hastened, 'I didn't mean from that angle. I was thinking of you, your own life. I always get quotations muddled up, but there's one about "how bitter it is to see happiness through another's eyes". You couldn't fool me.'

Anya felt her body sag, the strength go out of her, her will crumble.

'Not *bitter* in this case,' she corrected.

'Sad, then,' he said gloomily.

She didn't contradict; she couldn't.

10

MONICA returned to the hotel about five-thirty the following afternoon. Anya saw her, surprised that she was back, and aware suddenly that she looked extremely tired and pale.

'London was sweltering,' she said wearily, studying Anya intently as she spoke. Then: 'I'm glad you're here, Miss Rutherford, I wonder if you could spare me a few moments before dinner tonight? I'll order cocktails in my room. Come about six.'

Anya was about to make an excuse when Monica added: 'It's urgent and—important.'

'Oh. . . . Very well.'

Monica gave a faint smile, walked slowly to the lift and vanished.

Anya remained standing transfixed while the busy life of the hotel went on about her. Everything had become unfamiliar, remote. Noises came to her from a great distance, cars driving up and swinging around on the gravel drive; a motor mower chunking over the velvet lawns. . . . Monica! What did she want with her? Six o'clock. Her thoughts were disjointed. It was now five-thirty-five.

She knocked on Monica's door at about two minutes past six, her heart seeming to be the only sound in that long crimson-carpeted corridor. As she entered the room Monica smiled at her from a large armchair beside open balcony windows. Her feet were resting on a stool and she was wearing a négligé of orchid nylon which flared out gracefully from her slim, even thin, body.

113

'I'm so tired,' she murmured. 'Come and sit over here. . . .
This is a pleasant room, isn't it? Such a magnificent view.
I love this part of England.'

Anya had changed into a smart black dress, made certain
that her make-up was flawless, and yet in that second felt
at a disadvantage. There was something unnerving about
Monica's calm, her confidence.

Anya agreed, sat down, trying to stop her limbs trembling.
Between them stood a table on which had been placed a
salver with two dry martinis.

'I believe that is your drink, Miss Rutherford.'

'Thank you—yes.' Anya met that steady gaze without
flinching, trying to learn something from its expression and
failing.

Monica lifted her glass, nodded, drank and replaced
it.

'You're curious as to why I sent for you, aren't you?' She
paused significantly. 'And now you are here I don't quite
know how to begin, just what to say.' Anxiety clouded her
face. 'I thought it would be so simple, but . . .' Her head
dropped back against the cushions of her chair and she
sighed heavily.

Anya's heart was thudding, apprehension took the place
of curiosity and she said urgently: 'Mrs Latimer, just what
are you trying to tell me?'

'That I know about your relationship with my husband,'
she said startlingly.

Anya's eyes darkened with shocked surprise. Obviously
Guy had told her and the thought filled her with sudden
hope.

'The word relationship could be deceptive,' she said
quietly.

Monica's very blue eyes told Anya nothing as she replied:
'I appreciate that. But you are in love with him?' It was a
question which Anya had to answer and answer honestly.

'Yes, I am,' she said firmly.

114

'Do you genuinely believe that he is in love with you?'

'I think you can answer that question as well as I,' Anya said cautiously.

'That's true.' Monica sipped her drink again. 'I understand that you'd planned to marry once he'd got his divorce —on the grounds of desertion.'

'Yes,' said Anya resolutely.

'So that my return must have been a blow and a shock to you?'

'Yes,' said Anya again.

'And what are your feelings about the future now that you know—as I assume you do—my motive for returning?'

'Bewilderment, Mrs Latimer. Two and a half years is a very long while to remain away from someone you are supposed to love.' There was a note of sharpness in Anya's voice.

Monica counteracted it with gentleness. 'Is it impossible for you to imagine the courage it took to come back at all? The fear and the doubt lest Guy's love for me had died, or that he might refuse ever to forgive me?'

Anya dare not put out her hand towards her glass because she knew it would shake too violently to lift the drink from the table. And the sickness within her increased with the growing fear.

'No, that is not impossible. . . . But, what is the point of all this?' she asked urgently.

'To fight for a brief spell of happiness and to keep my husband with me.'

Anya cried out: 'Fight?'

'Oh, not in any unfriendly way,' Monica hastened, 'but because I know Guy, and that while at this moment I am quite ready to believe he is genuine in his love for you, I know, also, that he would not be happy to let me down— send me away. He's torn with indecision.' Her gaze was steady and honest. 'I represent marriage and all its ties. I'm his wife.'

Anya's hurt went so deep that she could not speak.

Monica went on in the same quiet, reasonable voice: 'He's a very fair, a very just man and even though I were to give him his freedom and he could marry you, he'd never really be at peace with himself.' Her words fell dramatically on the silence crashing into Anya's world like a death sentence. '*I represent marriage and all its ties. . . . I'm his wife.*' Seering facts lacerating her, filling her with a sick misery which nothing could remove.

She said with sudden courage: 'Mrs Latimer, if what you say is true isn't it inevitable that Guy will make his feelings quite plain—make the right choice for him? No one else can decide for him, after all.'

Monica answered with telling emphasis: 'If he had been sure—particularly of his love for you—do you think he would have needed any time to consider the matter?'

Anya's heart ached because there was so much truth, she argued, in that statement which she countered with: 'Couldn't that cut both ways? And since we are being completely honest, isn't it more a question of duty where you are concerned after a separation of two and a half years? Canada isn't at the other end of the world—a matter of a few hours' flying time. A man in love fights for the woman he loves. . . . Don't you think he would have followed you and tried to get you back?'

Anya was amazed at herself as she spoke and fully expected a sharp criticism but, instead, Monica replied: 'There is a very great deal in what you say. I am not trying to deny for one moment his deep regard for you; what I am stressing is the fact that, when it comes to a final choice, if he came to you he would not be a happy man. Already his attitude towards me has changed. The past has a pull, the experiences we've shared . . . the separation at this stage brings us closer.'

'Then if you are so confident of his feelings,' Anya murmured, 'why is this conversation necessary?'

'Ah.' Monica sighed. 'That's another matter. Just as Guy

has a loyalty to me, so, inevitably, he has a loyalty to you. He'd hate hurting you, but it would be a vastly different matter if you set *him* free. I know that then he would find happiness with me. Don't forget that, at heart, he is a conventional man and would detest the sordidness of a divorce case. My desertion would have made that phase of things simple for him.' She finished with conviction: 'And although if he shouldn't want to live with me again I am prepared to return to Canada, he'd never sue me on the old terms—knowing I was prepared to be his wife again. I'm sure you agree with me on that point.'

Anya said shakenly: 'Yes, I do agree. You talk of my setting him free. . .' Her eyes were round and dark in their pain. 'What did you mean?'

'That if you were to break with him, take the decision out of his hands, you would be giving him ultimate happiness and above all peace of mind. I know him so *well*. You could destroy him.' She put out a hand. 'No, don't misjudge me or resent what I'm saying. I know you're not a home wrecker, the ordinary type of other woman, or I'd not be talking to you like this.'

'I see,' said Anya dully, and it was as though the room had suddenly become dark and airless.

'Can you honestly say that you've been secure in your heart about his love for you in relation to me? To his marriage? Or that since my return you've not lived in suspense, fearing lest he might, after all, discover that I was the woman he really loved when it came to a final choice?'

Anya exchanged truth for truth.

'I'd admit all that, but I would add that I doubt if any woman on earth in such circumstances could be calm and absolutely confident.' She managed to lift the glass to her lips and drink from it. 'You had been a ghost to me . . . suddenly you became a reality.'

'A danger?'

117

'If you like.' Anya was struggling to shut out words that tormented her; trying to forget what had been said, clinging to the fugitive hope that Guy's love for her would be so overwhelming as to make it impossible for him to return to Monica and knowing, deep within her, that now even that would not be the end of the problem facing her so grimly, so shatteringly. Yet what proof had she of this woman's sincerity? Why should she take everything she said on trust? . . . As against that could she fault her attitude which had been both fair and conciliatory?

Monica said swiftly: 'I've hurt you and I'm sorry.'

Anya's voice was stricken: 'You talk of my setting Guy free. But he is free—free to begin his life again with you and equally free to—to choose to spend it with me. I should never—*never* try to persuade him. I've already told him that only he can decide.'

'And doesn't that prove my point yet again? That he needs to *think* about that decision?'

Anya shuddered. 'Haven't you yourself provided the answer to that question in his fairness and because he's the type of man he is? Wouldn't it have been out of character if he'd rejected you without giving the matter thought, but simply taking his own happiness?' Anya felt that she was running up a steep endless hill yet losing ground with every step.

'In one sense that is true; in another it bears out my contention that having rejected me and come to you, Guy would spend the rest of his life at the mercy of a conscience which never allowed him to be quite certain he was entitled to happiness. Would your future be secure on such terms?'

Anya cried wildly: 'They're just words in the circumstances. Why should he have a conscience when he takes into consideration all that happened, how you treated him . . .?' She knew even as she spoke that her heart and not her head prompted the outburst.

Silence fell; a dramatic, almost uncanny silence which filled the room more terribly than any sound. Monica's head again fell back against the pillows, she looked suddenly stricken, and older than her years.

Anya, frightened, leaned forward. 'Mrs Latimer, are you all right—you look . . .' She stopped as she met that very level, pathetic gaze.

'I hoped it would not be necessary to tell you this,' she said heavily, 'but the reason I am so sure that Guy would be at the mercy of his conscience is because I have only a year to live.'

For a second Anya stared at her allowing the full horror of her words to sink into a mind already bruised by all that had been said then, gasping, she cried: 'Oh, *no*.' And there was gentleness and sympathy beneath the terror of her voice.

'I'm afraid——'

'But,' Anya said urgently, 'there must be hope—nothing can be quite so certain.' And as she spoke she had forgotten in that moment her own involvement with the tragedy.

'I'm afraid this is certain. An unoperable condition,' she said starkly. 'A year is optimistic.'

Anya studied her with a new perception. . . . That fragility which had been obvious, yet not significant, now became symptomatic. Now her pallor was allied to a parchment transparency that tinged to grey. Outside the familiar sounds went on; the summer day taking to itself a poignancy as the shadow of a grim fate crept upon it, turning its brightness to twilight, its warmth to a cold clamminess that made Anya shiver.

'And you haven't told Guy,' she whispered, almost as though a normal voice was sacrilege.

'No, I haven't told Guy.' The answer seemed to come from a great distance and there was a faraway look in Monica's eyes. 'That would have been too much like blackmail.' She

119

paused and added quietly: 'So you see I'm really asking you for only a year.'

'But,' Anya insisted, 'shouldn't he be told? He'd want to know . . . I'm so sorry,' she added, aware that she had not expressed her sympathy in any specific words.

'I'd so much rather he didn't know,' Monica said firmly. 'It would lie between us, spoil everything and make it ten times harder for me. Perhaps in all this I'm being dreadfully selfish; perhaps I ought not to have returned to England, but I longed to come home; I was so tired of trying to be happy; so tired of loneliness. I've fought all this for so long. I had my first operation last year . . .' She added, catching at her breath, 'and I've had deep X-ray . . . I wasn't one of the fortunate ones.' Tears gushed to her eyes as she whispered: 'All this made me realize what Guy meant to me . . . in that dark world of suffering the word *husband* can mean salvation.'

Anya turned away and dropped her forehead against the palm of her hand for support, her elbow resting on the arm of her chair. Something died within her in that second; something that was hope, the future, happiness. When she spoke her voice had a note of strength, of dedication in it.

'Don't worry,' she promised, 'I will make the decision for Guy. I promise you that. I suppose in any case my heart knew you were right about all this.'

'I've hated it,' Monica said with a note of deep gravity. 'I can imagine how you feel, but there's just one thing, please keep my secret. I don't want Guy to know until he must. Then it will soon be over, anyway.'

Anya said urgently: 'But something fresh may be discovered; someone here in England might cure you. Look at the thousands of people alive today who were given only a short while to live. . . .'

'Mine,' Monica explained, 'is not a heart condition. I don't need to tell you what it is.' Her eyes were heavy and

120

sad. 'I've spent a fortune on doctors, both in Canada and America. London and Sir Richard Nonbury were my last hope. I saw him before I came down here. He could not reverse the verdict.'

Anya stared into space; she couldn't speak, but after a moment or two she said tensely: 'Will you answer just one question, Mrs Latimer?'

'If I can—certainly.'

'Then do you believe in your heart that Guy's peace of mind, his happiness—using that word in its widest sense—lies with you? That you are, even though he might not quite realize it, the woman he loves most?'

Monica didn't say anything for what to Anya seemed an eternity. Then: 'I believe that my return has made him realize the strange tie of marriage. Talking to him today—as I did—watching him, knowing that he hated the idea of letting you down and yet could not dismiss me . . . Yes, Miss Rutherford, genuinely I believe that provided he could *know you were all right and that you made the break* he would be rather like a man coming home to reality.'

'After having found a pleasant diversion with me,' Anya said, and for once could not keep the bitterness from her voice.

'That sounds cruel. . . . It's a question of *circumstances*. Had I not returned he would have got his freedom, married you and been able, no doubt, to wipe out yesterday because I had freed him. I left him, don't forget, not he me. I wonder if you can appreciate the subtlety of all this? The shades and degrees of emotion?'

'I think so,' Anya murmured, feeling ill with the pain of her own hurt. 'It's a very familiar story, after all.'

'Guy loved you, found happiness with you . . .' She hesitated.

'Because you were not there,' Anya finished swiftly.

Monica nodded. 'I don't think we could ever get much nearer the truth than that. It's odd, I don't want you to despise him, think him glib or insincere. He could not fore-see any of this and if he had less integrity he would not be in the state of conflict he's in now—torn, if you like—be-cause whatever he does he must hurt one of us.'

Anya's body sagged in the chair, strength ebbing from it.

'But,' Monica hastened, 'this is for such a little while—afterwards——'

Anya met her gaze very levelly. 'I'm sorry,' she said resolutely, 'I could not mould my life, my future, upon the possibility of your—your——'

'My death?'

'Yes.'

'I hadn't appreciated that angle, but I do understand it.' She sighed. 'I suppose I was thinking of his happiness and yours—afterwards.'

'We can't be sure of tomorrow,' Anya reminded her. 'All I pray is that your tomorrows may be far more numerous than you think. . . .'

Monica was so still just then that Anya felt she had passed to some world beyond her own comprehension.

'I don't quite know what to say to you, Miss Rutherford. . . . For hearing me out, for being so fair, so very courageous. I've asked almost the impossible of you, I know, and I'd like you to believe me when I say that, despite my circumstances, I would not have asked it unless I'd felt absolutely certain that Guy's true happiness lay with me. . . . Can you give me credit for that?'

'Haven't you given me credit for much the same thing?'

'You have made it very easy to do so.' She added with conviction: 'I think in the end you will live to thank me.'

Anya got to her feet. 'I have never wanted another woman's husband,' she said with conviction. 'I can only hope that your life will be so vastly different from anything you imagine now.'

The mellow light of evening rifted through that silent

122

room, falling upon the single bed with its green quilted coverlet. There were no more words to be said, but as Anya left and walked down the empty corridor to the main staircase, she knew that it was not only Monica who had been sentenced to death, and in that moment of agonizing misery she would gladly have changed places with her.

GUY raised his whisky glass and looked at James very levelly. 'Good to have you at Green Meadows, old man. Quite a while since you were here.'

'Work,' said James laconically. 'No social life these days. Lord knows why I went into the hotel racket . . . but you didn't ask me over to exchange pleasantries.'

'No,' Guy agreed.

'Monica?'

'Yes. I wanted to put you in the picture so that the facts won't get distorted before they reach you.'

James thought of Anya just then and there was a note of sharpness in his voice as he said: 'You're taking her back—reconciliation and all that?'

Guy looked deeply into the bottom of his glass as though expecting some curious shape to materialize. Then: 'No,' he said firmly, 'that's just it. I'm not doing anything of the kind. I'm in love with Anya and she with me. And I cannot convince myself that Monica has suddenly and miraculously had some great change of heart where I'm concerned, without an ulterior motive.'

'Are you asking me for my opinion—advice?'

'No,' said Guy firmly, 'because nothing could change my decision.'

'I'm delighted to hear it,' said James in his forthright fashion.

Guy's expression changed. He hadn't quite realized until then just how important it was to him to have James with him.

'Then that's settled.'

James took a gulp of whisky. 'I don't particularly care for a woman who makes a convenience and a mockery of marriage on the one hand, and then suddenly claims all its privileges on the other. And all the platitudes won't change my opinion.'

Guy nodded. 'Conscience can distort the facts in a situation of this kind. And it always appears to be so damned noble and virtuous to sacrifice yourself, until you realize that you are also going to crucify someone who not only loves you, but who has trusted you. I couldn't stomach being the married man playing the hypocritical forgiving husband for convention sake.'

'Thanks be,' James snorted. 'I must say it would have been out of character if you'd started something—made promises, shall we say, to Anya—without being absolutely certain what your feelings were for Monica.' His pause was significant. 'All the same, I wondered if you'd make the mistake of being loyal to the wrong woman—the woman who didn't deserve it—for no better reason that she used you and deigned to marry you.'

James was watching carefully as he spoke and Guy countered with: 'There's only one thing: in fairness, Monica appears to have changed—for the better.'

'I agree; but you can't be expected to live at the mercy of her inconsistencies. Life would be untenable on those terms.'

'Exactly,' said Guy.

'Does she know of your decision?'

Guy finished his drink. 'She should do, but I'm seeing her tomorrow.'

James puckered his brows, recalling Monica's words about meeting Guy in London and going back to their old haunts.

'Oh, I understand that you were to have seen her today.'

Guy lifted his head, his expression becoming faintly

surprised. 'I did see her—but not for long enough to go into any details.'

James was not going to allow Monica to get away with any deception. 'Did you meet by arrangement?'

'Yes—why?'

James relaxed. 'Nothing. I just wondered.'

'She telephoned asking to see me and I explained that I'd to go up to London on business in connection with the farm. As things worked out, I couldn't be with her more than a few moments.' Guy grinned. 'Any further questions?'

'No,' James said in his clipped, lilting tone. 'I'm satisfied.'

Guy said gravely: 'There are many things to be discussed and many obstacles to overcome.'

'You'll manage,' James said stoutly. 'When two people know what they want and how they feel, they work out their own destinies.'

'I agree.' Guy glanced at the clock. 'Anya's telephoning me at five.'

'I thought that clock had mesmeric powers,' James chuckled. 'And I must get going. Thanks for the drink at a time when we'd be dubbed alcoholics!'

'I needed a pick-me-up,' Guy said. 'London was sweltering today. I couldn't get back quickly enough. I'd only been in half an hour when I rang you.'

'You have my blessing,' James assured him. 'What do your people think of it all?'

'You know them. No interference and there was never any love lost between them and Monica. . . . I shall take Anya to meet them tonight. I'd wanted everything settled before I did that, but now the whole pattern has changed and it would hurt them to be shut out of something they knew really meant my happiness.'

James nodded his agreement.

He left just about five minutes before Anya telephoned.

Anya had ached to take the coward's way out and write to Guy, but she knew that she would despise herself for the

126

weakness. Nothing had been real to her since her talk with Monica the previous evening—nothing except her own unhappiness. She told herself over and over again that she was merely taking the initiative and sparing herself ultimate humiliation. Now, an hour after telephoning him—his eager voice still echoing in her ears—as she saw his car drive up at their appointed meeting place some short distance from the hotel, she felt that every vestige of courage, of strength, had deserted her. Only her love for him was real, her aching need of him.

He hurried towards her, holding her gaze, murmuring an endearment which she told herself meant nothing and was only a prelude to his announcement that he was going back to Monica. She must believe that; she must deaden herself to any hope that he loved her, Anya, above all else. . . . Unless she were cynical, even bitter, she would never be able to say good-bye, convince him that she did not love him after all. . . .

But the expression in her eyes precipitated his: 'Anya, what is it? What's wrong?' Fear touched him as he studied her pale, set face.

She plunged, knowing it to be the only way. 'Just us, Guy. The circumstances.'

As she spoke she heard the echo of Monica's words . . . '*I have only a year to live. . . .*' And again, '*Please keep my secret. . . .*'

'Oh.' Instantly he withdrew from her, the fact that no matter how great his love for her he was still not a free man, tying his hands behind him, making him sensitive to every phase of the situation from her point of view.

She didn't look at him as she rushed on: 'It seemed so straightforward before Monica returned. Now . . . We've both been forced to have second thoughts.'

'That's true,' he said gravely.

'I'm glad you admit it,' she murmured, emotion choking her.

127

'I admit nothing. You are doing the talking.' He would not, could not, help her because, as he stood there, it was as if his heart were cold and empty, his world about to disintegrate. 'But I take it you don't want to go on with me.'

Illogically, crying out for him to fight for her, unreasoning in her utter misery, she said: 'I don't believe in deluding myself. . . . You are married and your wife has come back.'

'I see.' His grimness was almost frightening.

'You——'

'Suppose,' he rapped back, 'you leave my feelings out of it and stop trying to tell me what I do, or do not, feel. The important thing is how you feel.' He stared at her disbelieving, feeling a terrible humiliation surge upon him because it was so obvious that she was not, after all, prepared to stand by him, and wanted to escape from their relationship.

Anya said: 'Let's—let's get in the car. We can't talk here.'

'No,' he agreed with cynicism, 'it is hardly the place for this type of conversation.

They got into the car and he turned in his seat to face her. 'Now.'

She clenched her hands one upon the other as they lay in her lap, trying to utter the words that would put him out of her life for ever, feeling so ill that she was afraid she would faint before her task was complete and then suddenly gaining the strength to say what must be said.

'I'm—I'm sorry, Guy—terribly sorry, but I'm going to marry Graham.'

For a moment there was a deathly silence while Guy stared at her, his face grim and mask-like. When he spoke his voice was icy and controlled.

'So that's the answer. *Graham!*' For an instant utter bewilderment flashed into his eyes. 'I must have been singularly blind.'

She cried out: 'No, it——'

'Don't,' he said hoarsely. 'There's no need to excuse your actions.'

She was trembling with misery, sick with emotion and her love for him. But she managed to cling to the last fragment of pride because it was all that was left to her. 'Is it so very different for me to marry Graham than for you to—to——'

He cut in bitterly: 'For me to be the married man.' A sardonic expression touched his lips. 'You're right, of course. I'm in no position to criticize or resent anything you do.'

Guy could not betray the hurt within him, he could not even fight, and integrity made it impossible for him to stress his own feelings. All he could offer in addition to his overwhelming love was . . . a divorce action, and even that would be fraught with difficulty. Graham, on the other hand, was free. Who could blame any woman for choosing life on those terms?

Anya rushed on. 'You and Monica will be happy again.'

Guy found it almost impossible to accept what appeared to him—despite the circumstances—a staggering change of heart. Anya had seemed to care so deeply. Their relationship had to him represented everything he had ever dreamed or wished for within the circle of human experience. And while at times fear and anxiety had beset him lest she might become impatient, dispirited because of the recent difficulties inseparable from Monica's return, he had dismissed them, believing that Anya was the type to live up to her promises and to whom inconstancy was foreign. He had, he told himself bitterly, been no better judge of her true character than, originally, of Monica's. Yet looking at her as she sat there, pale and silent, stricken almost, it seemed impossible to accept her decision, fantastic that in a little while she would go out of his life for ever and marry Graham.

He said in a weary, resigned voice: 'Happiness is a very large word—a very elusive, rare quality. I thought we had found it.'

'But,' she cried, unable to go all the way with her brave resolution and be detached from anything he might say, 'finding it when Monica was out of your life and—now——' Her sigh was heavy. 'You must *see*——'

'I do,' he countered, 'only too well. Of course you are right. It was an arrogant conceit on my part to imagine that you could be expected to care enough to bear this complication.'

His words lashed her because they were so opposed to her own conception of loyalty, and because she knew that there wasn't anything he could have asked her that she would not willingly have done. She could not keep back the words: 'You have a great advantage over me at the moment, Guy. . . .'

He exclaimed sharply: 'What do you mean? I should have thought that was the very last thing.'

'You were very uncertain of your own feelings when it really came to it.'

Even as she spoke, she found it difficult to analyse her reactions to Guy's attitude. It wasn't that she would have him harsh or uncharitable towards Monica, or even that she was so selfish she was blind to his sense of duty and responsibility in relation to his marriage. It was, in truth, the tormenting doubt lest that same duty concealed—perhaps subconsciously—an inclination to pick up the threads of their former life together and, thus, that same responsibility became a convenient cloak for far deeper emotions. Monica's own judgement remained to torture her. She could have faced up to a definite pronouncement that, after all when it came to it, his real love for his wife remained inviolate. Deprived of what she considered to be absolute honesty she floundered. Now she hung on Guy's answer which did nothing to ease the ache within her.

'Don't drag in my feelings in order to justify yourself.'

'I'm not trying to justify myself,' she insisted weakly, 'merely to put your viewpoint as well as my own.'

130

'Have I one—as you see it?'

'Because I cannot delude myself doesn't make me unfair.' She caught at her breath as she added: 'You will find happiness with Monica and—and——'

'You with Graham,' he finished for her sardonically. 'I must say you have worked it all out most conveniently.' He told himself that he had no right to undermine—even were that possible—her decision, or, for that matter, to tell her the truth about his own regarding Monica. But he could not beat down the searing jealousy, the desolation, the misery her dismissal brought him. He'd lived in a fool's paradise, believed what he wanted to believe, when all the time her feelings for him had been infatuation—an infatuation dying before one breath of reality and its attendant obstacles. Then, inevitably, Graham had come into his own.

Anya cried, struggling to cling to a fast-vanishing control: 'There really isn't much more to be said. I'd like to have felt you understood my point of view a little—as I should have tried to understand yours.'

He eyed her in amazement. 'You have an adroit way of twisting words. It is so very simple: You love Graham and you do not love me. Perhaps when it comes to it we have a good deal to thank Monica for,' he said, goaded by hurt and cynicism. 'Her return has brought us both to our senses and made us realize what a disaster our life together would have been.'

Anya felt that all the air had been crushed from her lungs. His words splintered around her like particles of glass, cutting into her flesh. Even if she could tell him the truth, betray Monica's trust, it would be a futile gesture. It was so obvious he would have returned to her in any case. He'd wanted life on his own terms. To play the self-sacrificing, noble husband, while endeavouring to convince her, Anya, that despite being forced to honour his obligations, he still loved her and wanted her love in return. It outraged his conceit to know that she preferred another man. He might even

131

have persuaded her—or tried to do so—to become his mistress. She was too sick, too nerve-racked, sanely to contemplate anything beyond her own hurt. Thus Monica's plea had been instrumental in shattering her world irrespective of the element of the original renunciation. Could anything be plainer than that final judgement of his: '*Her return has brought us both to our senses and made us realize what a disaster our life together would have been.*'

Her attitude changed, pride came again to her rescue, there was courage and challenge in her voice as she retorted: 'That being so, I hardly think you have any justification for putting on an aggrieved act because I am going to marry Graham.'

A great weariness surged over him and his reply was quiet and resigned. 'I'm not aggrieved, Anya. God knows I wish you all the happiness. . . . I remember very clearly what you said about Graham when we discussed our respective experiences that night at Green Meadows. . . . How long ago was that? Months or centuries?'

Green Meadows. . . . The mention of it made her heart ache with greater intensity. . . . Green Meadows. . . . Cool shadows lying like gentle fingers upon verdant, fertile land. The smell of new mown hay and honeysuckle, the ticking of a grandfather clock. . . . And dreams fading while the memory of them became so sharp that she felt the pain of death.

'Centuries,' she managed to say, adding with the absurd irrelevance common at times of tension and acute misery, 'And I remember your speaking of separate rooms. . . .' She stopped because only the vision of his making love to Monica was real to her just then. Now, with the reconciliation, those separate rooms would undoubtedly become one.

He didn't speak and his silence fed her belief that all her suppositions about his feelings were true. That left only platitudes.

She felt his gaze upon her, pointing her lips almost as

though he were lost in contemplation of them, making her aware of his kisses, of their past, their hopes, their dreams. For a second courage flagged. Suppose, even now, she told him the truth? Did she owe Monica loyalty? Suppose he still cared for her, Anya? And that he was playing his part as she was playing hers, so that one breath of appeal from her might put back the clock to yesterday. . . . Self-contempt and scorn mocked her weakness. Had he said anything calculated to convince her of his love for *her*? And even had that been so . . . She knew she could not smash Monica's life—or what there was left of it—break her promise. Her sigh was heavy as she murmured: 'I must go, Guy. I'm sure you've no desire to continue this conversation.'

'No,' he agreed stiffly and there was a cold, withdrawn look in his eyes. 'There's nothing left for us to say to each other, Anya—nothing.'

'We seem to have done most of our talking like this—in the car,' she murmured hollowly, realizing that this was the last time she would sit there beside him and that when they met again—if ever they did—it would be as polite strangers.

'I suppose that's true,' he said, depression washing over him. He couldn't grasp the fact that this was the end of his hopes, that in a matter of minutes she would be lost to him. Graham. . . . She must always have loved him, for he recalled her honest admission that she had done so *once*. . . . That love had obviously never died and with the complications surrounding his own affairs, flared back to life. Well, it was useless arguing; useless piling hurt upon hurt without achieving any constructive purpose. 'Can I,' he asked politely, 'drive you anywhere?'

She shook her head, too unhappy to speak, and then looking at him remorsefully. 'Human relationships,' she managed to murmur, 'are very strange. . . . how quickly they can alter, how swiftly yesterday loses its meaning.' Her words lashed him and she realized that it would be impossible, in

133

any circumstances, for him to appreciate the sense in which she had meant them.

'That,' he answered icily, 'rather depends on the type and character of the relationships, their depth and their integrity.'

Anya didn't speak, but made a gesture conveying her intention of getting out of the car. Immediately he slid from his seat and opened the door for her.

'Good-bye, Anya,' he said, and his voice was so still, so expressionless that every nerve in her body ached for the comfort of his arms, the old weakness returning, courage dying. This was the end. Finality.

'Good-bye, Guy,' she whispered. 'I hope you and Monica will find your happiness again.'

She did not give him an opportunity of replying—even had he been disposed to do so—but turned and hurried away, not looking back in case will power deserted her.

Guy watched her, bereaved, his heart thudding, misery and desolation mingling with jealousy and wounded pride. How anxious she had been to make her point that he would return to Monica when, formerly, it had represented, naturally, that which she most feared. Even then he could not bear the inevitable conclusion that hers was the facile, inconsistent attitude, and that he, himself, had never been more than an interlude. He started the car up, jammed in the gears and tore off down the empty deserted road. It didn't register that he was driving in the opposite direction from Green Meadows. Time, place, everything in his life had disintegrated.

12

Anya met Graham the following evening at The Speech House in the Forest of Dean. He knew by her expression that she was unhappy and anger made him snap: 'Now what's that fellow done? You look——'

'Please, Graham. . . . Let's have a drink and talk afterwards.'

'Very well,' he said uncompromisingly. 'Shall we eat here?' Instantly he answered his own question. 'I know—you don't want to eat anywhere. Suits me. I'm not exactly feeling hungry myself. . . . Dry martini?'

'No.' It was too reminiscent of Guy. 'Sherry.'

'But you dislike sherry.'

'I may do, but I prefer it this evening.'

They drank in silence, then: 'Let's get out of here,' Graham said restlessly, leading her through the hotel—thought to have been a hunting lodge used by Charles II—to the entrance where his car was parked. She stood for a second looking at the long winding road cut through the forest with its magnificent trees of all descriptions, its peace and its pungent earthy fragrance. It seemed suddenly that she had no home, that all her roots had been torn up, her future mutilated. Guy had represented home, purpose and her life. Without him there was nothing.

'I have,' said Graham, 'a flask of coffee and sandwiches, we can find a pleasant spot and picnic.'

She flashed him a grateful look.

'I knew by the tone of your voice over the telephone that

this was hardly in the nature of a celebration,' he added somewhat grimly.

'That will rather depend on how you, personally, look at it,' she countered.

They turned off to the right by the old Roman road—now a pathway of flagstones—and found a little clearing in the forest where Graham parked his car, spread out two rugs, and brought a picnic basket from the boot. They settled comfortably and Anya broke the rather awkward silence with: 'Graham, you once asked me not to shut you out of my life whatever happened. Do you still feel the same way?'

He lit a cigarette. 'Certainly. I'm not the changeable type.' He looked stubborn. 'It's Latimer, of course.'

'It has been,' she said so quietly that he stared at her in amazement, the past tense making his heart lighter than it had been for a very long while.

'You mean——'

'If I ever see him again it will be by accident.'

Graham felt a mixture of relief and annoyance. It was so obvious how deeply she had cared and still did care.

'I'm glad you've come to your senses,' he exclaimed admonishingly. 'I suppose his wife put a stop to it all.'

'You could put it like that,' Anya answered.

'What did I tell you,' he said almost gleefully. 'I always warned you he was no good. They always go back—these philandering husbands—after they've had their fling and made some poor deluded mistress unhappy.' He chose his words deliberately. He had to know the truth and couldn't bring himself to ask the question. A statement often achieved the same result.

'I was *not* his mistress,' she countered instantly and with annoyance.

He turned to her. 'Sorry, Anya. But the whole thing— what I didn't know and what I suspected—just got too much for me.'

136

She made a little sympathetic gesture. 'You can't tell me anything about hurt,' she said, but there was a note of defiance in her voice.

'So it's over.' He stared out across the forest now rifted with the evening sun which touched it with golden fingers, giving the scene a stereoscopic effect.

'Yes.' She knew she must tell him as near the truth as possible. 'He was going to divorce his wife for desertion; her return——'

'You don't need to explain.'

'It isn't just as you think. There are other factors. I got out, Graham.'

'I admire you for that; and I'm glad you spared yourself the humiliation of being dismissed. I heard from Mrs March that he'd met his wife in London yesterday and that they'd been reconciled.'

'That,' said Anya hotly, 'is not true.' Monica would not have found it necessary to appeal to her had that been so. She shivered. That appeal, after all, could still have been a further insurance for the future. Double security. The thought, while not changing the situation or the circumstances, stabbed her. 'I doubt if Mrs March could speak without putting her own interpretation on a thing.'

'Be that as it may—he will go back I take it.'

Anya sighed. 'Yes,' she admitted, 'although he did not say so.'

'That doesn't surprise me. It's much more comfortable to sit on the fence and get credit for loyalty which isn't there. I tell you I know these cases backwards.'

'I'd much rather not discuss them, Graham. I'm trying to be honest with you.'

'I know you are, but the sound of that damned fellow's name makes me see red. . . . I don't need to ask you if he put up a fight for you.' His cynicism made him vicious because of the jealousy that prompted it. 'I'll bet he was thankful to be let off so easily.'

137

She bristled. 'You don't help me to be honest. I hate you when you talk like that.'

'My dear, the truth always hurts, but if you don't face up to it now you never will. And you can't expect me to think more of him because *you* got out and saved him the annoyance of telling you that he was going to be the noble self-sacrificing martyr and returning to his wife, but that, of course, he'd always love *you*. Bah! Makes me sick.'

Anya shivered in the sunlight. It might have been winter she was so cold. She said, the words rushing out: 'I told him I was going to marry you.'

Graham gave an exclamation of amazed delight. 'Marry *me*,' he echoed. '*Anya*.'

'Oh, I know it was presumptuous, but it was the only way to resolve the situation. I had to make it all absolutely definite. Now I realize that I'd no right to bring your name into it——'

'You'd every right,' he insisted brightly, 'that is if you'll live up to the statement.'

She stared at him and even though she had half expected such a reaction it was a still a shock.

'But that would be horribly unfair to you.'

'It would be damned unfair if you refused to stand by your word.' He added complacently: 'I always knew you would marry me in the end, anyway. It was the waiting that was so hellish. Oh, Anya, if you could realize what you mean to me. . . . There's never been anyone else—never. There never will be.'

It was ironical, Anya reflected, because that was just the trouble. Graham, to her, despite his intelligence, his success, was not wholly a man living in a man's world who had shared a man's experiences. His wisdom was obtained through observation and not because he, himself, had suffered to obtain it.

'But,' she said firmly, 'very well, so long as you know I'm not pretending, marrying you under false pretences.'

'And now that I'm not in the dark about Latimer.' He looked at her searchingly. 'I'll take that risk, darling.'

Darling. . . . And Guy's eyes meeting her, the echo of his voice as the word died away; a word holding magic for no better reason than that he had uttered it. She murmured, hoping she did not sound as dejected as she felt: 'I'll try to be all that you want me to be, Graham. In time——'

'I'm not a bit afraid,' he interrupted, 'that Guy will come between us. In your heart you know him for what he is.'

She had no inclination to argue. 'Daddy will be happy,' she said irrelevantly. 'He always wanted you in the family.'

'Son-in-law as well as partner. What could be better?' His eyes were bright and full of confidence. 'And with Loreli in the picture everything's going to be fine.'

They had talked without emotion, without Graham making any attempt to kiss her and she was grateful for the fact. Now, however, he leaned forward and put his arms around her, bending his lips to hers. She tried to respond and to avoid hurting him by any coldness, but it was as if all feeling had died within her, her body marble instead of flesh and blood.

'When,' he asked, drawing back from her, 'will you marry me, Anya?'

'Next spring,' she said firmly. 'I'd like to keep on working until then.'

'With Fawcett, still?' He shot the remark at her.

'Yes.'

'I'd rather you were further away from Latimer.'

She made a little scornful sound. 'Two miles or two thousand, the result would be the same. Her gaze was steady and honest. 'I'd loathe it if you didn't trust me.'

'It isn't that. I know his type. Having gone back to his wife, he'll then try to worm his way——'

Anya didn't allow him to finish as she rapped out: 'And do you imagine I'd tolerate anything of the kind assuming your deductions are correct?'

'Do you question them?'

'No.' She was hesitant.

'I tell you,' he said, and there was an almost violent note in his voice, 'that all these married men are the same——'

'Perhaps. *I* am still an individual, though. Don't lose sight of that fact or we shall quarrel.'

Graham stared at her. It was amazing how firm and challenging she could be. Even in these circumstances he could not hope that she would be malleable clay.

'Of course,' he hastened. 'Very well—April next year. I wish it could be next month.'

'I'd like time to adjust myself and to plan ahead, Graham.'

'That's reasonable enough. . . . We'll build our own house,' he added cheerfully. 'I've always promised myself that. I like security. None of your hit-and-miss lives for me, darling.'

Anya made no comment, but she knew that with Guy she wouldn't have cared if he'd been penniless.

They parted at the hotel later that evening.

'We'll tell the family at the week-end,' she said. 'Daphne will be home and Loreli will be there.'

'The week-end being tomorrow,' he said with a smile.

Time had ceased to mean very much to her.

'Of course . . . I'm off in the evening and have Sunday as well.'

He held her gaze. 'I can't quite believe any of this,' he said solemnly. 'I think I'm afraid you'll vanish.'

She shook her head. 'Don't be. I'm very real and very solid.'

'All seven and a half stone of you!'

She stood beside the car as he returned to it, having seen her out.

'Thanks, Graham—for everything.'

'Thanks for giving me almost everything,' he replied quietly. 'I know I'll win in the end and I'll collect you around six tomorrow. Will that be right?'

'Just right. . . .'

He drove off and she went into the hotel.

James was standing in the hall smoking a last cigarette before, as he said, 'turning in for an early night'. She had not seen him to discuss any personal matters since her parting from Guy.

'How about having a walk in the gardens.' He looked at her speculatively.

'And the early night?'

'That was before I'd found you to talk to,' he grinned. 'I don't know, suppose we skip the walk and have a drink instead?' He beckoned a waiter as he spoke and there was a note of authority in his voice which made it unnecessary for Anya to do more than agree to his suggestion. They went into his untidy, book-lined sitting-room, their drinks were brought and they settled comfortably in the two deep armchairs. James raised his glass and said: 'To you and Guy. I'm so damned glad that things have worked out for you.'

Anya stared at him. 'I don't quite follow,' she murmured thinly.

James didn't hesitate. 'I mean about the future,' he explained confidently. 'The fact that Guy wasn't going to be fooled a second time by that wife of his.' Something in his expression made him stop abruptly. 'Or am I putting both feet in it?'

Anya put down her glass, every nerve and muscle in her body seemed to be taut. 'No, no of course not.'

'Splendid,' said James in his customary jargon. 'I must admit I was thankful when Guy told me that nothing would make him give you up—or words to that effect. I suppose I was afraid he'd get some foolish notion about duty into his head.' He grinned again. 'I underestimated him. Shrewd fellow, Guy. Can't catch him *twice*.'

Anya gave a little cry. 'You mean that—that Guy told you he wasn't taking his—his wife back?'

'Yes. He told me when he got back from London. . . . But

141

you know all this.' His gaze was suddenly alert and inquiring. And in that second the telephone rang. James answered
it. Then: 'Guy. . . . Hello.'

Guy said briefly: 'James, that matter I discussed with you
yesterday . . . Regard it as a confidence, will you? I was
making a fool of myself when I imagined Anya shared my
feelings. She's going to marry Graham Collins.'

'What?' James almost roared.

Guy gave a little bitter laugh. 'Only goes to show that it
doesn't do to delude oneself. I'll be over in the morning.'

James replaced the receiver, his movements almost trance-
like. He'd already betrayed the confidence without any
breach of good faith. Now what? He eyed Anya with a keen,
half critical eye.

'Now I begin to understand your attitude,' he said
sharply. 'You're going to marry Graham. . . .'

Anya sat there, bleak and miserable. 'Yes,' she said, and
there seemed nothing she could add to the admission.

'Guy didn't want me to mention his decision . . . Since I'd
already betrayed his confidence to you without realizing
what had happened——' He added swiftly: 'But he wasn't
speaking in confidence yesterday, his whole attitude was—
good God, Anya—why? Why, suddenly, Graham?' He
shook his head. 'Do you realize what you've done to Guy—
what this means to him?'

Anya remained immobile.

'He will live to thank me,' she said firmly.

'That's sheer hypocrisy,' James exploded. 'You don't
know Guy; you can never have known him.'

Anya tried to conceal the agony within her, to conceal
the wretchedness and shame she felt because she had mis-
judged Guy so dreadfully. She couldn't pretend, or make
excuses to justify herself. From the start, beginning with her
mother's words, she had been so afraid of hurt that it had
distorted every truth, undermined her faith, made it so easy
for her to believe that, when it came to it, Monica would

take precedence even though he professed not to care for her. How he must despise her now for her attitude. She ached to rush to him, to implore his forgiveness, but what would that achieve in the circumstances? Nevertheless a terrible doubt began to build up in her mind . . . If *Guy* refused to listen to Monica, to believe in her, how could *she* be certain that the story of her illness was true? And that being so wasn't she, in all probability, the victim of her deceit?

Anya looked at James and her stillness unnerved him; it was out of character in the circumstances.

'I will admit that, if it will enable you for just one moment to hear me out, James. Do you believe deep down—cutting out false sentiment in every way—that now I'm to marry Graham, Guy will take Monica back?'

James made a faintly impatient sound. 'How can I answer such a question?'

'Very well, I'll ask you another. . . . Do you trust Monica? Do you believe that if Guy were to take her back she would make an effort to see that he was happy?'

James shuffled in his chair, then got up restlessly.

'I dislike the woman; I'm prejudiced against her and admit it. But if I try to be fair—which as Guy's friend isn't too easy—then I'd be inclined to say yes. When Guy told me how he felt about you I was delighted. I'd been so afraid lest he wouldn't see the wood for the trees, and I still maintain that there's no earthly reason why he should consider Monica; why he should condition his life to her whims when she walked out on him as she did, having married him for purely material reasons.' He shot Anya a reflective glance before adding: 'I wouldn't have said this to Guy, but I've a feeling that Monica came back because she's not as fit as she used to be. There's just something about her—a look, if you like.'

'Are you suggesting that you think she is a sick woman?'

'Not exactly that. Merely that she is a tired one, who has found that a husband serves a good many useful purposes.

She would not have come back unless it was for her own ends. I'm not deceived,' he finished, 'but——'

'You wouldn't take a lease of her life,' Anya ventured breathlessly.

James snorted.

'Only the good die young! Nothing dramatic like that. It's an instinct—something you women have,' he admitted.

Anya didn't speak. This was a question which only time would answer and if Monica had been telling the truth . . . Anya felt rather like a person giving to a dozen beggars in case she missed the one deserving case. She could hardly demand from Monica proof that her life was forfeit and certainly no medical man would commit such a breach of etiquette by betraying his diagnosis.

'Would you say that normally—in the past—she had been a very persuasive woman?' she asked tentatively.

'Frankly, no. She wasn't the type to persuade. Demand, yes. . . . But why the cross examination?'

'No particular reason.'

'And isn't it rather late in the day for it, anyway?'

Anya answered quietly: 'Yes James, it is.'

He said impatiently: 'I just don't damned well understand you.'

'That isn't surprising,' Anya retorted, 'I don't understand myself.' Her gaze was steady. 'In the circumstances, would you rather I looked for another job?'

'Heaven forbid! I've said my piece. Guy's my friend and I can't pretend I like to watch him fooled and made unhappy. What's more I gave you credit for integrity.'

Anya's voice deepened. She leaned forward and there was a great earnestness in her voice as she pleaded: 'If I told you that I was still worthy of your faith, James, would you believe me?'

'You make things damned difficult, woman,' he exclaimed roughly.

'I've made many mistakes—I know that—but they've

144

been human and not treacherous ones. I've learned a bitter lesson that love and fear cannot go hand in hand yet, contradictorily, that is precisely what happens and fear wrecks and distorts. Or it could be that a general verdict on a matter of precise circumstances blights the truth.' She made a little helpless gesture that was endearing. 'None of that can make sense.'

'Oddly enough,' said James flatly, 'it does. You were the last girl in the world to fall in love with a married man. It was not only against your principles, but your nature. I'll take a level bet that you always lived in torment lest Guy didn't really love you, but still loved his wife.'

'Isn't that,' she flashed at him, 'the theme song of all these affairs? That after a passionate, soul-stirring interlude the man suddenly and miraculously discovers it is his wife he loves—often for no better reason than that his comfort or position is in jeopardy?'

James gave a faint chuckle. 'You paint a graphic picture.'

'Shall I quote you?'

'No. . . .' He raised his hands in an almost comic gesture of fear, then suddenly became serious. 'I've answered all your questions, will you return the service?'

'If I can.'

'Are you still in love with Guy?'

The room became suddenly silent; a heavy silence that took from them both the façade of pretence. Anya had no desire, or intention, of lying as she said quietly, yet with a deep sincerity: 'Yes, I am. I cannot imagine that there will ever be a time when I cease to love him.'

James flopped down in his chair. 'But it doesn't make *sense*!'

She flashed back at him: 'How much of life—or of human conduct—does?'

'We're dealing with you.' His gaze became critical. 'And what of Graham? Hardly——'

145

She interrupted. 'I am not deceiving Graham.'

'Then that just about makes everything crazy,' he retorted. 'For heaven's *sake*, Anya. I presume you must have a reason for all this.'

'I have,' she said gravely.

'And if Guy should find out?'

'He will never do that and'— her eyes were challenging in their steady gaze—'you will not betray this confidence because I ask it as a point of honour—no matter what the circumstances.' She paused for his answer.

'Oh, all right,' he agreed grudgingly. 'The whole thing is beyond me. . . . Do I tell Guy that I'd already discussed things with you before he rang?'

'Please—*no*!'

He shrugged his shoulders. 'It's all so baffling.'

'I know, James. . . . Do you mind if we say no more? All I ask is that you don't misjudge me entirely.'

He gulped the remains of his whisky.

'I suppose I must accept all this on your terms.'

She got to her feet. 'Please. Time will solve the problems, believe me.'

'And if Guy and Monica do start again?'

'Then there'll be no problem—obviously,' she said quietly.

'I don't like any of it.'

'Neither,' said Anya, 'do I. Good night, James.' The silence that fell between them had the curious quality of sympathy. He broke it as he opened the door for her and said vehemently: 'Perhaps one day I shall be told something that makes sense.' But even as he spoke his contemplation of her was full of solicitude. He liked Anya and nothing would ever convince him that she was capable of disloyalty.

'I doubt it,' Anya murmured.

He held her gaze deeply and penetratingly. 'How about taking a few days off—just to get your breath. You're due for the week-end, anyway, and we could manage for two or

146

three days extra. By then, I rather imagine, Monica will have left.'

'For Green Meadows,' Anya said, her reaction instinctive. The thought of Guy's love for her, his loyalty, was like a throbbing wound in her heart. She felt unworthy of it even in the present circumstances.

'Who can possibly answer that question? But be that as it may, I'm going to insist on your getting away from here—you're too valuable to lose and at the rate you're going now you'll be in hospital!'

Anya grinned. 'I must look charming . . . I would like to have those few days. Thanks, James. My sister's coming home for the week-end and there are all manner of things happening in the family.' There was a wistful expression in her eyes. 'Also, it's only fair to Graham to have time to celebrate,' she added, her voice low and curiously sad—the sadness of resignation.

'Then that's settled. I'll see Miss Colby.'

'Hardly fair to——'

'Colby thrives on work—particularly since you've joined us. She likes you, Anya. A staunch ally that. Trust her implicitly. *And* she isn't blind.'

Anya said irrelevantly: 'You're a pretty wonderful person, James. Why don't you marry and give some woman happiness?'

He laughed. 'Because no one will have me.'

'That's absurd.'

His attitude changed. 'If you lose the right person, it isn't easy to compromise. I lost the right person. . . . Oh, Anya, think well before you marry the wrong man.'

'I have, James. My reason is valid since he is not being deceived.'

'I wasn't thinking of him,' came the grave reply. 'Good night, my dear. Get away early tomorrow and relax as much as you can.'

'I feel I'm running away.'

147

'Nonsense; we're so well organized here nowadays—your department runs so smoothly—that coping will be easy.'

Anya gave him a little grateful smile and hurried away. She couldn't bear the compassion in his eyes.

13

IT WAS the following Tuesday that the Rutherford celebration took place. They chose an old Regency hotel near Ross-on-Wye for dinner and dancing. Marcus, gay and smiling as he sat at the head of the table, exclaimed: 'I never thought that this kind of evening was possible.' He looked at Anya and Graham, then to Daphne and Paul (whom he'd accepted, believing in his integrity so far as ultimate marriage to Daphne was concerned and wise enough in his enlightenment to realize that his opposition, in any case, would serve no good purpose whatsoever) and, lastly, with a lingering tenderness at Loreli, sitting on his right. 'All of us—here together.' He looked back at the wine list. 'Only Champagne could do justice to the occasion.'

Anya gave a little gasp. Her father had never drunk it, or thought in terms of it.

'Pol Roger, 1947,' Marcus said, half to himself and then to the wine waiter. 'No. 4.'

Daphne shot Anya a staggered glance. Was this the man they'd regarded as a pompous mountebank and whom they had, in truth, almost disliked? Now, he looked ten years younger, as though suddenly and miraculously he had found an enchanted garden and all the lost joys of a previously barren life. . . . Loreli crystallized for him all the shy dreams of youth which had eluded him, and in maturity those dreams had become reality. Anya thought bitterly how often people resented the things denied them, and in their resentment grew hard and remote. . . . Would that happen to her?

149

Would her love for Guy, and the overpowering need for him, break her in the end?

She glanced at Graham, flushed with pride and obvious happiness; at Paul, quietly confident, the man in authority knowing precisely where he was going and making it perfectly plain that Daphne was going with him. He was the last man she would have imagined Daphne choosing. An intellectual who loved ideas rather than solid facts, and who detested triviality and the jibbering idiots who mouthed platitudes believing them to represent conversation. Yet he was not superior but very human; he would infinitely prefer the honest-to-goodness labourer to the dreary-minded. With him Daphne was a different personality, her flippancy, her brittleness, gone. In security, in the knowledge of his love—proved beyond doubt—she allowed every facet of her character to shine. Anya thought of words said by whom she could not recall: 'A woman is beautiful when she is loved.' It had never been truer than in her sister's case. But to it she would have added: 'provided, also, that she returns the love'.

Loreli, mysterious and yet contradictorily naïve, in soft black with a diamond spray for relief, smiled across the table as a mother might have smiled at a beloved family of which she was obviously a part. Already she *belonged*. Her relationship with Marcus was as natural as though they had been married for years instead of merely engaged for a few days. There was a strength about her, a confidence, which brought out in Marcus all the attributes that had been smothered for so long. Loving had made them both young, not because they were romantics living in an illusory world, but because they were realists who had discovered that everyone's existence was bounded by the depth and understanding of the love encompassing it. Anya reflected that it was the effect of one human being upon another, the degree of their harmony and attunement, which dictated which attributes flourished or withered. In the case of her father and mother (beyond the ties of family and home) there had been nothing to weld them into a complementary, satisfying whole; they were always two people working on entirely different wave lengths. If she mourned anything it was the fact that her mother, unable to stimulate or awaken reciprocal emotions in the man she had married, had died without having ever known happiness or fulfilment. Her father was living to experience both.

She wondered about Paul's wife—who she understood was desperately anxious for her freedom, finding life with a man of his calibre intolerable. They had married in immaturity only to find that, after the first sharp passion was over, they had nothing whatever to say to each other. Anya was glad to know that Mrs Ross, in turn, had her future planned with a man whose love of routine and domesticity would atone for the lack of both in Paul.

Graham said: 'Just where were you then, Anya?' A note of jealously crept into his voice.

'I was thinking about Paul,' she said honestly.

Paul looked at her with interest. 'Why?'

'You're the first writer I've ever met.' She studied his dark, well-cut hair and well-groomed appearance. He wasn't good looking, but there was a vitality and scholarliness about him which she liked.

'My hair is short,' he suggested with a broad smile. 'And I don't throw fits!'

Daphne flashed him an adoring look. 'You're just normal enough to be excitingly abnormal!'

Graham said rather stiffly: 'Someone must come down to earth.'

Paul smiled without effort. 'I never could quite see why coming down to earth suggests virtuous solidity while imagination is always suspect. I'd like to think the two could meet and serve an excellent purpose.'

'Seeing that you live by your imagination,' Graham said rather deprecatingly, 'that is natural.'

Anya wasn't listening, she was hearing sounds which appeared to be miles away from her and then suddenly everything around her was lost as she saw Guy standing at the door of the restaurant, Monica at his side, as the head waiter indicated the table to which they were escorted. It was not until Guy was seated at the far end of the room, and in direct line with Anya, that their glances met, and the silence beat around them as though they were the only two people there.

Anya saw the swift regretful looks that flashed from Daphne to Paul and the sudden dark fury that crept into Graham's eyes. She tried to think of something to say but, as on all such occasions, failed. Graham might have been arrogating to himself the right to speak for her.

'And so another marriage stands the test. . . . That makes five reconciliations I've been in on this week. Not too good for our business.' He added hastily: 'But the general rule.' He saw the resistance in Paul's eyes. 'Sorry. . . . There are always the exceptions.'

Marcus said rather curtly, irritated, although at one time Graham could do no wrong: 'I don't think we're particularly interested either in the Latimers' affairs, or the morality of marriage.'

Anya shook so violently that she had to clench her hands beneath the table cloth and press her arms against her body to prevent the fact being noticed. She was not able to fight against the jealousy that tore through her.

Daphne said sharply: 'Because a man has dinner with a wife from whom he's separated, it doesn't follow that they are about to become turtle doves.'

Paul changed the subject.

The meal proceeded. Every now and then Anya looked across—as though drawn by a magnet—to Guy's table. She noticed that Monica did most of the talking. Guy sat there, sphinx-like, inscrutable. What was he feeling, thinking? Did he hate *her* for what he could only believe was her fickleness?

152

Or did some memory linger to haunt him? Womanlike she loathed the idea of his suffering on her account and yet ached for the balm of knowing she still meant enough to inspire it! She didn't look as the champagne cork popped, but the sound faded out as she heard Guy saying: *'I have never drunk champagne like this before, darling.'*

Just then her eye caught his and she saw the bitter cynical curl of his lips, followed by a sudden weary resignation as he turned to Monica.

Anya struggled to eat the meal, her stomach resenting every mouthful and making her feel sick, the champagne burning her mouth. The possibility of making a scene by having to get away from the table rather than to faint as she sat at it, appalled her. The restaurant revolved nauseatingly. If only she could get away. But that was impossible and somehow she got through to the coffee stage. Later Graham said, as they danced on the small square of parquet—around which the dining tables were set and lamp-lit—'Latimer doesn't appear to care for dancing.'

Anya flashed him a warning glance. 'Isn't it possible to talk of something—or someone—else?'

Graham exclaimed roughly: 'I loathe his being here tonight.'

Anya sighed deeply. She understood so well. 'Oh, my dear, please don't hurt yourself so much.'

'You love him,' he said aggressively. 'Don't you?'

Her gaze was steady but patient. 'Would you prefer I lied to you?'

'No.' He drew her closer.

'Listen,' she rushed on urgently, 'you accepted this position, Graham, without my deceiving you. Oh, I know I'd no right to have said we were engaged——'

'You'd every right,' he protested, 'you knew how I loved you.'

'Yes,' she said gently, 'but have I the right to hurt you as I obviously seem to be doing? Don't you see? Am I asking

153

in this situation more than you can bear? Heaven knows I don't want to do that. . . . Yet if one accepts, really chooses——'

He interrupted her.

'Let me say it for you: if one accepts a set of circumstances in order to achieve one's dearest wish, one cannot then rail against those circumstances.'

'Or blame the person honest enough to warn you of them before you committed yourself,' she added forcefully. 'I can't stand atmospheres, Graham, even though I can understand and appreciate your reactions; but bitterness and resentment will not make our relationship to be bearable.'

He looked shamefaced. 'I didn't know I was so jealous,' he admitted frankly.

Her gaze was searching. 'I shall never betray your trust.'

'I know that.'

'Very well then. Let's not mention Guy again, or rather, if we are unfortunate enough to haunt the same places, don't make it an issue.'

'I promise,' he said humbly.

She added to that: 'Are you sure you want to go on with me?'

'*Anya!*' He sounded horrified.

'I'm serious, Graham.'

'So am I, darling. Of course I want to go on with you. Haven't I always wanted this?'

'Yes. . . . Give me time, Graham, and in the end I may be able to make you happy.'

'I'm happy now.' He looked around him. 'You're my fiancée. People know. I'm identified with you.' There was pride in his voice.

It was just as the dance was ending that Anya noticed Monica making dumb signs to her, indicating a doorway leading to the Ladies' Powder Rooms. As the music stopped, Anya, baffled, her heart racing, managed to get away, giving Graham a meaning smile as she left his side. She waited in

154

the semi-circular lobby from which both lavatories and hand basins radiated in their respective compartments. Long mirrors and wall dressing-tables, well lit, were far more reminiscent of a London hotel than a country one. After a few seconds of suspense in which Anya's mind darted from one unlikely thought to another, Monica appeared.

'I had to have a word with you,' she said in a low, appealing voice.

Anya studied her with a brutal objectivity. She looked ill beneath the expertly applied make-up and there was a forlorn air about her. As always she was beautifully groomed but the black dress accentuated her pallor.

'Why?' Anya asked without any undue sympathy.

'Because some of the things I told you that—that evening have proved not to be true. I've done a good many shabby things in my life but . . . to appeal to you as I did in any way under false pretences——' She broke off.

Anya's heart felt that it was hanging at the base of her throat, choking her.

'What do you mean?' she asked breathlessly.

'That but for your obvious sacrifice—your engagement— I doubt if Guy would have considered taking me back. I thought he was very much the typical married man type. I didn't know him. I flattered myself that when it came to it he would discover that I mattered most . . . I was wrong.' She looked at Anya very steadily. 'I can't think of any other woman in your position who would have behaved as you have done or been so—so generous. I may be jealous of the love Guy has for you, but I am grateful to you—so *grateful*.'

There was a poignancy in her words and her attitude that killed the last remnant of Anya's doubt.

'Please,' she said sympathetically, 'that's all over.'

'You've given me that *reprieve*.'

Anya tensed. She could not escape the implication of that

remark. And suddenly she had to know, to put an end to conjecture.

'Meaning that——'

'Guy has agreed to a reconciliation,' she said quietly. 'I returned to Green Meadows today. At least now we understand each other, can speak the same language. For the short time left to me I believe we shall be happy,' she added. 'I think I was afraid of being alone to face things.' Her voice shook.

Anya turned to her then and said urgently: 'Mrs Latimer' — the word had a foreign sound but she hurried over it— 'don't you think you should tell him the truth?'

Monica heaved a sigh as she shook her head. 'If I did that he would probably never forgive me.'

'But—*why*?' Anya sounded outraged.

Monica looked down at her hands, pensive and a little uneasy.

'Because then he might guess I'd told you—used the fact to take you away from him.' She paused eloquently. 'Which has, after all, been true. I don't feel very proud of myself,' she added simply.

Anya had a curious sensation of wretchedness which had nothing to do with her feelings for Guy, but rather was mixed up—ironically—with his for Monica. Now his judgement of her, his scepticism, his refusal to believe she had changed, seemed harsh and uncharitable. Who could possibly doubt the sincerity of a woman who was ready to admit her mistakes, to put herself in the wrong entirely? This discounted even the remotest possibility of that being true. She said quietly: 'I shouldn't think about it any more. Something in Monica's downcast expression made her add swiftly: 'And Guy, after all, didn't *have* to begin his life with you again. The fact that I was out of the picture was not——'

'Oh, I see all that . . . I just feel rather mean. I've come back and, in effect, spoiled everything for you.'

Anya felt a lump rise in her throat.

'You have every right to this happiness,' she murmured, and all the warmth, the humanity that was an integral part of her true character, surged to lend great sincerity to her words. 'Genuinely I hope it means——' She was going to speak in terms of the future and stopped.

Monica put in with a wry smile: 'All I ask is to prove in this year—prove to Guy—that I love him.'

'You will,' Anya said encouragingly.

'And you?'

'You know my future. It isn't important.'

'I think it is. When will you marry Mr Collins?'

'Next April.'

'Must it be so soon?'

'I cannot *use* him . . . Having promised . . .' Her words were abrupt and she did not attempt to finish the sentences, but added: 'In any case'—her gaze was fixed steadily upon Monica's face—'I refuse to believe the sentence passed upon you. There are numberless people who have been through your experience only to live to a good age.'

Monica said sombrely: 'That may be so, but look at me . . . can you do that and repeat those words?'

Anya gazed into Monica's curiously magnetic eyes which beneath her make-up were ringed with dark shadows and she shivered. There was something about her; something which no power could explain, and yet which struck dread into Anya's heart because 'that look' seemed to be a death knell.

'You see,' Monica said quietly.

'No.'

'Do you believe in miracles?'

'Yes; they happen every day,' Anya flashed confidently, 'particularly when people believe in them. That above all.'

'I'm afraid I don't,' Monica said flatly.

People crowded into the make-up room, shattering the moment of silence.

Anya felt the poignancy of that moment as though Monica were outside the circle of her own life.

157

'But——'

Monica interrupted: 'All the same, thank you for everything.' She moved to the door as she spoke and even as she opened it, Daphne came blithely through, nodding pleasantly as Monica allowed her to do so.

'What,' Daphne said to Anya a moment later, 'was her affable smile in aid of?' Her gaze was solicitous. 'Has she been talking to you?'

'Yes.'

Daphne looke astonished. 'That means she had done so before—that she knows *of* you?'

'Yes,' said Anya again. 'I'll tell you everything one day, Daphne. At the moment it is best this way.'

'I understand, but now, being happy myself, I—I hope I'm a kinder person, Anya, and you've been wonderful to me.' She stopped and there was a look of consternation in her voice as she asked: 'Is *she* living at Green Meadows again?'

Anya nodded, then: 'Heavens I need some powder; my face shines like a full moon.' Her laughter was high-pitched and mirthless.

'Mine too,' said Daphne. She began her make-up and then said abruptly and irrelevantly: 'You know, I don't like her.'

Anya, sitting at the next mirror, turned. 'Why?'

'Not prejudice. There's just *something*. I've a feeling she'd never miss a trick. It's her eyes. I'm not usually the observant kind, but just now I saw an expression . . . triumph's the word. No, it isn't prejudice.'

'She hasn't anything really to be triumphant over,' Anya said quietly.

Daphne pursed her lips and said: 'Um-m,' then went on with her lipstick.

Anya came face to face with Guy later that evening as she walked across the dance floor to get her stole, before the party returned to Wyvern.

'Good evening,' he said in a crisp, impersonal tone.

She murmured something inarticulate, her gaze meeting his in what was a sub-conscious appeal. Would he stop and had she the courage to force him to do so? For a second they hesitated, then she managed to add smoothly: 'This seems to have been an evening of universal celebration.'

Guy both loved and hated her in that minute; hated her for the pain within him; loved her for all she had stood for in his life; even to look at her at she stood there, brought an aching loneliness.

Graham reached them with the swiftness of an arrow finding its mark.

'Hello,' he said pleasantly. 'So you and your *wife*'—he stressed the word—'have found this unusual hotel. Delightful, isn't it?'

'Very,' replied Guy.

Monica came towards them from the hall entrance, ready to leave. She inclined her head graciously towards Anya and then Graham as Guy made the introduction.

'I believe we have a mutual friend, Mr. Collins—Sylvia March.'

'For my part an acquaintance, Mrs Latimer.'

She smiled, and looked up at Guy, who said abruptly: 'Ready?'

'Yes . . . good night,' she murmured.

Guy held Anya's gaze for an instant, his expression chilling and bitter. 'Good-bye,' he said significantly.

Graham rushed in tactlessly as he and Anya were left alone.

'Made it pretty plain that so far as he was concerned he didn't want to see you again. Bad loser I'd say.'

Anya didn't speak, merely shot him a silencing glance.

The party broke up, the couples driving off in their respective cars.

Marcus reached out rather shyly and touched Loreli's hand. 'A good evening,' he suggested, rather than stated.

'Wonderful.'

'Happy?'

'So happy, darling.'

Marcus flushed, the endearment was new and exciting to him. Neither he nor Harriet had used it during the whole of their married life.

'I feel quite confident about Paul, don't you?' he said swiftly, and because emotion was rushing through his body alarmingly.

'Quite; I like him. They'll be well suited, he and Daphne. Utterly different, but a complement to each other.'

'No need even to mention Graham and Anya. I always knew she'd choose him in the end. Good chap, Graham.'

Loreli didn't speak, but she asked herself indulgently why men were so blind on occasion.

14

THE months passed and September and a rich harvest kept
Guy busy. Long golden shadows crept over the fields, soft
gentle mists hovered in the valleys, the trees flanking the
lawns of Green Meadows were brushed with copper, burnish-
ing them almost as though lacquered. The light was sharp
and yet in its sharpness there was a magic which touched
every blade of grass, every flower.

Guy looked out upon the scene as he sat opposite Monica
at the breakfast table, and the hunger within him deepened
because it fed on his loneliness and love for Anya which
separation had merely accentuated rather than subdued.

Monica said petulantly: 'Guy, can't we go up to London
for a few days?'

He transferred his gaze from the garden to her. 'I can't,
Monica. Why don't you go if you feel like it?' He was
mechanically opening the letters that lay on his plate and
tossing them aside because they held no interest.

'Would you mind if I did?'

He knew that he would be thankful for the respite. The
past months had been a strain. Monica had, he admitted,
been pleasant and undemanding, but they were two strangers
sharing a common roof; polite, considerate, without
emotional contact at any level. What puzzled him was the
fact that she had accepted the pattern without seeking to
alter it. The doors of their separate rooms remained shut,
and the possibility of this order of things changing had
never been mentioned. She had not embarrassed him by any
impassioned pleadings for his love, or stressed her own. He

was grateful for that; grateful also that she had not even wished for Graves and his wife to change their routine and had not—as he had expected—asserted her authority and a former arrogance, to spoil the harmony and smooth running which he had previously enjoyed.

He answered her swiftly. 'Not at all. . . . You've friends to go to?'

'Yes.' She looked at him. 'We're rather a unique couple—aren't we?'

'Perhaps the circumstances are unique.' He dreaded any discussion of an emotional nature.

'Do you ever see Anya Rutherford?' Her words broke up the silence.

'No. I've not seen her since that night at the hotel when——'

'We started again together?'

'Yes.' He was slitting open envelopes as he talked.

'I've tried to live up to our bargain, Guy.' Her voice was low and a little tremulous.

He raised his eyes to hers. 'I appreciate it. But for the life of me I cannot see why you should prefer being here like this.'

'I gave you my reason when I returned. It hasn't changed. I hope you might feel differently by now.' Her calm was almost unnerving.

Guy felt the terrible weight of indifference crushing down upon him. He could look at her, appreciate that she had charm, was an elegant woman; he could accept the fact that she had endeavoured to live up to all she promised. Now he would not like deliberately to hurt her, but there was no emotion whatsoever in his reactions. He realized that indifference was the cul-de-sac of all relationships. A stagnant unfulfilment devoid of hope. Hate was a positive, vital force which could be transmuted into love; indifference was negation; a lost point of contact. Even if his love for Anya could die, there was nothing he could do about Monica. He said honestly, 'I warned you about all this.'

She nodded and studied him through half-closed eyes. 'You are a very strange man, Guy.'

Something in her tone made the air electric, superimposing upon his indifference all the old distrust, the suspicion, that had never left him despite her attitude.

'No doubt.'

'And must you go on reading your letters?' she said, her voice raised almost to a shriek.

Guy had just flicked open a crisp sheet of writing paper, his gaze flashing across the typewritten words. Watching him she saw his expression change, his mouth harden to a fierce anger. She gasped: 'Guy, what is it? What's the matter?'

'Nothing except that I've opened a letter intended for you.'

Her eyes widened in horror. 'For me,' she gasped. 'I don't believe it, I mean I——'

'You mean that you *over*looked this one,' he said icily.

Graves brought more coffee in that second, and staring at him, at his immobile face, Monica trembled. Graves smiled to himself. His loyalty, he insisted, was to the master and he hadn't liked the way Mrs Latimer rushed ahead of him for the post and went through it, searching nervously for handwriting he had come to know, if not well, at least well enough to recognize. And on this occasion he had been just one move ahead of her, keeping back that particular letter from the afternoon of the previous day, in order that he might insert it in the master's correspondence that morning —*after* she had looked at every envelope brought that morning!

'Give that letter to me,' Monica shouted, when Graves left them.

Guy tingled with a strange excitement—half contempt, half satisfaction—because he had been proved right.

'I'll do better than that. I'll read it to you,' he said, and his voice was bitingly cynical.

Her protests were futile as he read aloud:

163

'*Dear Monica,*

I'll be in London at the flat on Friday and shall expect to see you. Unless I get my money back within seven days I shall sue you and then your husband would know you'd returned to him because you were penniless. I've stood the racket long enough. This is final.

H.B.'

Monica had got up from her chair and reaching Guy's side, ripped the letter from his grasp. Her face was distorted with anger. Guy's sudden icy calm both frightened and subdued her and she cried: 'I'm still your wife.'

'You are still Mrs Latimer,' he corrected. His gaze was steady and unnerving. 'So that's the answer, the truth,' he said slowly. 'I always knew there was something wrong with the picture of your playing the contrite wife . . . I must confess this angle had never occured to me.' The thought of Anya seared him. . . . Yet whatever happened between himself and this woman made no difference to the fact that Anya had preferred another man.

Monica sat down. She felt sick.

He said, amazed: 'What on earth did you do with your money?'

Colour burned in her cheeks. Every nerve tingled with a hatred nothing could wipe out.

'So,' said Guy, 'it was a man.'

'Clever—aren't you?'

'No, Monica, if I had been I'd have stuck to my guns and never let you inside this house again.'

Monica summed up the situation swiftly. Anger would get her nowhere.

'Everything I said to you was true,' she insisted. 'But I didn't mention the money in case you would not believe me.'

At that he laughed. 'Give me credit for a little intelligence.' His voice was authoritative. 'And now suppose you tell me

164

the facts? If you don't I shall be forced to make my own inquiries.'

She moved and sagged into an armchair, letting her head fall back against the cushions.

'It was someone—a man in . . . Real Estate.' Watching her Guy saw the sudden pain that came into her eyes. 'I—I liked him, trusted him.'

'And gradually transferred your money to him for investment,' Guy said sardonically. 'Rather out of character, wasn't it?'

'No.' Her hands tightened on the arm of her chair. 'That money meant everything to me, and he was one of the most reputable men in the town. He made money for many people—people I knew. I'm not the only woman who wants all she can get—higher interest rates than the measly sums paid on so-called safe investments. He had a legitimate business to begin with . . . in the end he lost all he possessed and all his clients possessed. I hope he rots,' she added fiercely.

'Was he your lover?' Guy's voice was so cold and impersonal that she was taken off her guard.

'Yes,' she flashed back.

'And you cared for him?'

The room took to itself a strange vacuum-like unreality, as though it were nothing except echoes, memories, mind pictures.

'Physically, yes. Otherwise no.'

Guy lit a cigarette. He was completely detached from anything she had said so far as their relationship, or the past, was concerned; what burned within him was the fierce resentment, the bitter knowledge that, through her, his own life had been wrecked irrevocably.

Monica knew that she would gain more by being honest and appealing to Guy's generosity, than by fighting him without weapons. That *letter*. A fury raged within her. She knew that Graves had slipped it into the pile on Guy's plate

165

knowing that it would be slit open mechanically—as was Guy's custom.

'And you talked of returning to Canada—all that nauseating hypocrisy when all the time you'd . . .' He made an impatient gesture as though the whole thing was beneath his contempt. 'A marriage certificate can be very useful—almost a blank cheque,' he rapped out.'

'I don't deny it.'

'And this—this letter? Where does *he* fit into the picture?'

'I borrowed money from him to come home with.'

'Which you intended to get out of me?'

'Yes.' Frustration surged over her. She'd counted on Guy being malleable clay on their reconciliation, giving her sufficient power to achieve her own ends, but his coldness, his refusal to live with her had made any approach about money dangerous.

'You *must* have taken me for a fool,' he cried.

'Perhaps.' Her voice was brittle. 'I didn't count on Anya Rutherford.'

'We're not talking of Miss Rutherford.'

'No? Well, we shall have to do so,' she exclaimed cunningly. 'After all, I've been honest with you about my—my life.'

'That doesn't mean I have anything to tell you about mine,' he snapped.

Monica changed her tone.

'I should think it very odd if you and she had not been lovers. I'm more than ready to admit that I've treated you pretty shabbily.'

'That's damned decent of you,' he roared, his temper rising. 'My God, Monica, I knew you were no good, but *this*—this loathsome act to get back here . . .' Words failed him.

'Security,' she said, 'is pretty valuable when you've lost it.' There was fear in her eyes. 'Don't you see, Guy? I'd been ill and alone——'

'Don't expect me to sympathize,' he cut in.

'What else could I do?'

'There's such a thing as work.'

'I tell you I wasn't well enough to work.'

His gaze flicked over her like a whip. 'And now?'

She looked down at the letter, frantic because her world had crumbled with those few sentences. The 'Dear Monica' cutting into her heart. For Hugh to have written *that*. . . .

'I don't know,' she said weakly. 'I don't know.'

Guy stubbed out his cigarette. 'And you've no more tricks that will deceive me. Looking pathetic, raving, threatening—they're all the same to me.' He added with a deadly calm: 'You can get out of here—today. I flatly refuse to go on.'

Her face was white; her eyes wide and hunted. She jumped out of her chair. 'No,' she cried shrilly, 'no . . . Guy, you must listen. . . .'

'I suggest you get H.B. to listen.' His gaze was full of sudden loathing. 'You've smashed every hope of happiness for me; you destroyed everything when you returned here. . . . And all the time it was money . . . to be kept . . . to use me so that in the end you could betray me again.'

She stumbled towards him, clutching the lapels of his jacket.

'Guy . . . I know; I know, but let me stay here . . . I——'

He tore her hands from him and thrust her aside. 'Spare me the melodrama.'

'But what shall I do? Where shall I go? I'm your wife,' she said desperately, and now all fight had gone from her; she was the coward grovelling and he was sickened by the sight.

'It's a pity you didn't appreciate that fact before,' he said curtly, and before she could reply he strode from the room.

She sat there shivering with fear. . . . The letter mocked her and she crumpled it into a ball and flung it across the room. Graves came in, his face mask-like as he began to clear the breakfast table. Monica looked at him and all the

167

pent-up emotion, the frustration of having her plans foiled, found an outlet in her savage cry, 'You did that deliberately, didn't you?'

Graves turned an inscrutable gaze upon her; his voice was maddeningly polite as he asked: 'Did—what, madam?'

She clenched her hands and then shook them in her violence. There was nothing she could do, nothing she could say. . . . All her carefully worked-out schemes had failed. And in that second she thought of Anya and the lie she had told her; the lie upon which the foundations of her present life at Green Meadows had been supported. . . . A sudden gleam of hope came into her eyes. Guy could say and do what he liked, but she was still his wife and the next move would be up to him.

15

GUY got into his car and drove away from the farm. He felt homicidal. Fool ever to listen to Monica, to take her back even as a wife in name only. Yet having lost Anya life seemed so futile that he was utterly indifferent to whether or not Monica was in his house. His actions had been the measure of resignation, the line of least resistance, certainly never of any change of heart, and while it had *appeared* that Monica was a different person, nothing that had happened surprised him. Had this not been so he would have taken her back in the beginning without question and as a duty. Now, he asked himself, what lay ahead. His car seemed to turn automatically towards the hotel. He must talk to James. . . .

But James was not there, having gone to Cheltenham. Guy stood disconsolately in the hall, glancing towards the reception desk, but Anya was missing from her accustomed place and he wandered out into the garden, aimless, unable to fight against the tumult within him. Suddenly he saw her as she stood, basket on her arm, cutting flowers for the tables. At the sight of him she stopped and involuntarily, her gaze lingering in his, cried: 'Guy.'

'I came to see James,' he said flatly, lost to everything but the fact that she was there, her dark eyes meeting his in a sudden wordless appeal, which made it seem that his love for her was beating in every nerve and pulse of his body.

'I expect they told you he'd gone to Cheltenham,' she said, managing to keep her voice steady.

'It's a long while since we met,' he murmured abruptly. 'That night at the hotel.'

To Anya the time had seemed eternity. She had looked for him in every face that came through the hotel doors, in every street, knowing that to see him would achieve no good purpose, and yet craving it above all else. Just to *see* him. . . . Had he forgotten? Had he turned to Monica and then lost himself in *her* love? Torturing, tormenting and unanswerable questions beating mercilessly in her brain.

And suddenly the tumult stopped; suddenly for both of them the peace and loveliness of that September day and their overwhelming need of each other were one, and all the problems, the heart-ache vanished before the wonder of being together again. Guy hesitated a second and then reached out towards her, scattering her basket and her flowers as he drew her into his arms, his lips meeting hers with all the passion of love denied, finding in her response an answer that stirred every emotion of which he was capable. They were lost to time or place as they clung together in a frenzy of ecstasy and swift desire. To Anya it was as though the world had disappeared leaving her floating in some enchanted sphere where there was nothing beyond the magic of his touch, his kiss and the heavy thudding of his heart against her breast.

And as they drew apart, thoughts rushed up at Guy from the dark recesses of his mind so that irrelevantly, almost sharply, he said: 'Monica . . . where did *she* fit into the pattern that parted us?'

Anya tried to master her emotions sufficiently to be coherent, to grasp the full significance of what he said.

'I—I don't understand.' Her eyes, starry in her flushed excited face, met his.

'You love me,' he said triumphantly. 'Whatever has happened, you *love me*.' He spoke as though nothing beyond that could ever really count.

'We've no right,' she hastened. 'Guy, this is madness——'

'This is truth and our *life*,' he said solemnly.

'Monica and Graham are also truths.'

170

'Graham, yes,' he admitted, and felt the knife of fear turn in his heart. 'Monica'—there was distaste in his utterance of the name—'is a lie. I always knew it and I was right. *Right*,' he repeated with a bitter emphasis.

Anya shuddered. 'No . . . Oh, no! That would be too ironical.'

'Why,' he demanded, 'did you send me away—become engaged to Graham? Anya, I must *know*.'

She stared at him in bewildered uncertainty, then she said in a dull, hopeless voice: 'Knowing will not change anything.'

His gaze travelled over her face, resting finally upon her lips caressingly. 'If you can tell me you're not in love with me, that these moments were just an emotional impulse, and that you truly love Graham, then there's no more to be said. . . .' His voice trailed away only to rise again as he insisted, gripping her shoulders as he spoke: 'I don't think I could believe you, even then.'

She looked up at him, her eyes filled with a tenderness that was the measure of her love.

'You know my heart,' she whispered. 'I can't betray it a second time.'

'Then *why*?' He added almost fiercely: 'There must have been a reason and Monica was behind it.'

'It was a good reason, Guy. It still is.'

'I'm not going on with her, Anya. Everything about her is false—utterly false. Now do you see?'

'But I don't follow . . . what has happened?' There was a note of fear in her voice.

He told her the truth, finishing harshly: 'Now do you realize why I must know the rest of the story?'

Anya couldn't absolve herself from a promise so easily.

'All that, Guy—horrible though it is—doesn't really change the situation for me. It could be argued that everything Monica has done was the result of the facts as I know them. . . . And why are you so certain that she parted us?'

'Trust,' he said simply. 'Trust in you. Suddenly seeing you here . . . I don't know. . . . All the tumult and the conflict died down. You're a part of me and only jealousy, hurt and my own invidious position allowed me to let you go in the first place.'

'Oh, Guy,' she murmured piteously, 'if only I could have believed you had absolutely no love for Monica . . .' She added swiftly: 'It wouldn't have prevented my finishing things between us, but it would have prevented my becoming engaged to Graham.' There was a shining light of honesty in her eyes. 'If only love weren't so hurt by its own possessiveness.'

'I still,' he insisted, 'want to know why you finished things.'

Anya's gaze met his very solemnly. 'If I refuse to tell you, would you——'

He cut in sharply: 'I have finished with her, Anya. Finished. What my position is so far as a divorce is concerned, I don't know. But I do assure you that if I were never to see you again I am determined not to share a roof with *her*—and sharing a roof,' he said meaningly, 'is all our "reconciliation" has meant.'

They moved and sat down on a rustic seat nearby. She held his gaze in a wondering, half questioning look as she said: 'I promised Monica I wouldn't betray her confidence.'

He exploded. 'So I *was* right.'

'Yes. . . . She told me she had only a year to live.'

For a second there was an uncanny silence which Guy broke with a bitter laugh.

'And, being you, you believed her?'

'Yes.'

He flashed instantly: 'Yet believing that you became engaged to Graham.'

Anya flushed. 'Because I believed, also, just what I told you a few moments ago, that when it came to it, your true

172

affection lay with her. Graham was my only weapon . . . the one weapon you could not fight.'

Guy sighed, a deep, hopeless sigh. 'How she *could*,' he said distastefully.

Anya looked back over the incidents of the past months. 'She seemed so honest, so open about everything.'

'She can be that . . . so convincing. Don't I *know*.'

'She made me believe that——'

'That if given time, etc., etc., I should be grateful to you for getting out, so that my precious marriage remained intact?'

'Yes.'

'Monica never misses a trick.'

'No,' agreed Anya, recalling the conversation she had with her at the hotel that night. 'She even admitted to me afterwards that she had been wrong about your feelings and *thanked* me for giving her this year.'

'My God,' Guy muttered, 'it doesn't seem possible.'

'She wanted that year to consolidate her position financially.'

'Precisely. Only H.B., whoever he is, became impatient. The one flaw in an otherwise perfect scheme.' His voice dropped. 'What are we going to do, my darling?'

She said tensely: 'I can't just use Graham—even though he knows how I feel—and then leave him because the situation has changed.'

'No,' Guy agreed, 'you can't do that.'

They looked at each other almost in panic, feeling the bleak desolation of an empty future rushing up at them.

'I think,' she said shakenly, 'I can bear anything now that you understand; now we are sure of each other. It was the barrier between us, the knowledge that you could only have despised me.'

'But,' he cried roughly, 'my darling, how could you believe her? The whole *thing*——'

Anya's lips quivered into the ghost of a pitiful smile. 'And hadn't she convinced even you that she'd changed . . . everything she said, even the way she *looked*, made it impossible to disbelieve her and one wouldn't *dare*.'

'If only I'd realized.' He leaned forward and let his hands drop loosely between his legs. 'All I could see was Graham,' he admitted.

'And all I could see was—your *wife*,' she added quietly.

'Love makes its own hell.' He looked at her. 'Do you believe now that there has never been anyone else for me—not even for a second? That everything I said to you when she came back was tied up solely with that hateful word, *duty*?'

'Yes.' She spoke in an almost ashamed whisper.

He put his arm around her shoulders and held her closely.

'Now I feel so helpless, so hopeless and,' he added violently, 'so bitter.'

Anya's voice shook.

'How could anyone—anyone tell such dreadful lies. And she *acted* the part that night, Guy. She looked so ill.'

A gleam of near hatred came into his eyes.

'Monica can look and be anything,' he said harshly. 'But I'll admit I didn't think she'd stoop to that. If only I'd suspected . . . Oh, what's the use, all the self-condemnation won't change the facts.'

'No,' said Anya gravely. She was thinking of Graham, knowing that she could not break away; that ironically she felt more morally bound to him than she would ever have done had she believed she loved him in the beginning. As it was, to let him down now would be like dishonouring a debt. 'You see, when I told you I was going to marry Graham he was unaware of the fact.'

'Oh, *no*,' Guy groaned, his expression desperate in its frustration.

'I knew that he wanted to marry me and that I couldn't fight against you without using his name.'

'In order to give Monica security,' Guy said, and there

174

was a terrible anger in his voice. 'It was a diabolical thing for her to have done.'

'Yes,' said Anya and shuddered. 'Could *anyone* have challenged facts like that?'

Guy met her gaze very levelly. 'Perhaps they could have demanded medical proof. . . . Perhaps you would have done that, had there been less conflict within yourself.'

Anya said, sick with regret: 'That makes it even harder to bear. When one can find reasons to blame oneself—one's lack of trust . . . Guy, forgive me—forgive me for doubting you, for thinking of you so much as the married man. I was wrong—dreadfully wrong. Monica's part in it all doesn't absolve me.'

'My dear,' he murmured gently, 'if we always did the right thing, and were less the victims of our emotions, there'd be no light and shade——'

'And no tragedies.'

'If only I could fight for you; if only I could tell you how wrong you were about Graham. But I can't.'

Anya gazed around her, helpless against the tide of passion, of love, that surged through her. This was finality and it was useless denying it.

'What will you do?'

He shook his head. 'Without you—does it matter? I've told her to get out . . . but without money where can she go?' he asked, and there was gentle irony in his tone. As for getting my freedom . . .' He sighed heavily. 'And what would freedom be without you, in any case?' There was a moment of silence before he added: 'I couldn't hope to get *evidence* against her and her word'—contempt quivered in his voice —'she'd deny anything to suit her own purpose.'

'Which is to stay married to you,' Anya murmured, and there was inevitability in the utterance.

'Exactly.'

'This is good-bye,' Anya said, with sudden terrible inevitability. 'We both know it.'

'I love you,' he exclaimed, and there was passion in his voice as though he were defying fate to separate them.

'And I you. That at least is left to us.' She got to her feet, the tension unbearable; the awareness of him, of their mutual need, making words futile and meaningless. Her heart felt bruised, her body hollow.

'Darling—*darling*,' he said hoarsely.

'Don't, or I shall cry,' she pleaded. 'Just go—quickly.' Her voice quivered into the silence and at that moment they heard footsteps and saw Graham striding almost militantly towards them.

'So,' he said icily, 'this is where you are, Anya.'

Anya, managing to keep back the tears that stung her eyes, smiled. 'That sounded like heavy melodrama.'

Guy said politely: 'Good morning.'

Graham looked through and past him, turning to Anya. Guy hesitated, met Anya's appealing gaze, murmured good-bye, and, turning, left them.

'What was he doing here?' There was a challenge in Graham's voice.

'He came to see James.'

'And found you. Very convenient.'

Anya's heart felt that it was being torn out of her body as she watched Guy's receding figure. . . . In a second it would be lost from view and from her world. Even the thought of Monica, and of the trick she had played, failed to weigh against the misery and depression seeping into her, which left no place for anger. It was too great. But on the heels of that came the overwhelming, tormenting thought: if only she had behaved differently; refused to believe Monica and placed more trust in Guy. . . . Trust. . . . How many women in their time had said just that. . . . How many lives been wrecked on those pathetic little words, 'if only . . .'

'I thought,' she managed to say to Graham, 'you were in court today.'

'The case was postponed. I hoped you'd be free this afternoon. I've to go to Chepstow.'

Anya was grateful that she had a genuine excuse.

'I'm sorry, but Una Colby's off and I'm doing part of her work.'

'Queer kind of set-up here.'

'It works,' she reminded him.

He said suddenly and irrelevantly: 'Anya, couldn't we get married before Christmas? I hate this waiting. It's hell.'

Anya knew that there was no escape and she said with a quiet confidence: 'Very well, Graham—if that's what you really want.'

He stared at her, amazed by her answer. He'd expected protest and argument.

'*If* it's what I *want*,' he cried with sudden excitement.

She studied him intently. 'But are you sure?'

He said half-accusingly: 'Sure because you still aren't in love with me—that's what you mean, isn't it?'

'Yes,' she admitted quietly. 'I can't deceive you.'

'I think I almost wish you could.'

Their glances met and she understood.

'What *was* Latimer doing?'

'It was an accidental meeting.'

'Oh.'

'I'd not seen him since that night at the hotel.'

'Suppose his marriage should go on the rocks? Although I doubt if she'd ever divorce him.' He might have been talking to himself as he added: 'And she strikes me as the type to make sure he could never divorce her. I've seen her about with Mrs March. Just *something*——'

'Yes,' said Anya, sick at heart, 'something.'

Graham shot her an inquiring, half-suspicious look.

'What do you know . . . what was he saying?'

Anya cut the last flower and put it in her basket.

'There's nothing that need be discussed . . . I don't want

177

to talk about it again.' She was firm and he knew the subject was closed.

They walked back to the hotel together.

.   .   .   .   .

When Guy returned to Green Meadows later that day Monica was sitting idly on the sun porch. She looked up at him rather arrogantly.

'What are you doing here?' he demanded, fury smouldering into flame.

'I live here,' she retorted. 'You daren't turn me out—like some old-fashioned melodrama—without any money. I'm your wife; your pride, and your prestige, is at stake.'

'I'm going to divorce you,' he said icily.

'Really? On what grounds?' Her laughter tinkled. 'What I've *told* you. I'd deny every word and I was always very discreet. The man was married. . . . No, Guy; you'll never divorce me and I shall never divorce you. Better get that into your head. If you want me to leave this house you'll have to pay me to do so. It's as simple as that. A man must keep his wife; fail to do so and I'll sue you. When it comes to it I've all the weapons.'

'Such as you had with Miss Rutherford and the lie you told her. . . . The lie that——'

'That wrecked all your cosy little hopes, your precious dreams. And you talk of divorcing me! Why, I'd drag her into it all and make you both sorry. In fact I could start something pretty nasty *without* the help of the divorce court. . . .'

He looked down at her disgusted, incapable of stooping to fight with her.

She laughed. 'If you want a scandal you can have it at any time. So suppose you come down off that high horse. I'm not leaving here until I've enough to pay my debts and something to live on. I know the law pretty well, Guy. . . . That's

178

why I came back and foiled your little plan about divorce. Sylvia was very useful in warning me about your interest in Miss Rutherford. *She* was the biggest stumbling block.'

'You're beneath contempt, Monica.'

'I know. But I get what I want—or part of what I want. You'll pay me rather than share a roof with me, my dear man.'

Guy knew that was true.

'Whatever the arrangement it will be made by my solicitor,' he said sharply.

'Fine; I don't care if it's made by your dentist . . . I heard a morsel of news, by the way. Your dear Anya is being married in November. Sylvia saw Mr Collins this afternoon. They're going to Madeira for their honeymoon. And Marcus Rutherford is marrying his young widow next month.' She sighed languidly. 'I get all the latest news.' Her gaze fell with studied insolence upon him, moving upwards from his feet to his smoothly tanned skin and dark eyes which met hers with a merciless contempt. 'Funny you don't attract me, isn't it? You're really quite a fine specimen of a man.' She stifled a yawn. 'On the other hand being your wife has distinct advantages. I intend to keep them, so if you've any ideas of finding some other mistress . . .' she sniggered, 'and don't expect me to believe that dear Anya was never that—it won't make a scrap of difference. I still shouldn't divorce you. . . . No, Guy, having studied our respective positions I'm rather satisfied with mine. I panicked this morning . . . I didn't realize just what power a wife has.'

'For evil,' he rapped out.

'If you like.'

'And the money you owe? If it isn't paid——'

She smiled, a slow, cunning smile. 'It will be. You'd hate your name dragged into all that sordidness through me. I should tell such a pathetic story. After all I convinced Anya that I was a dying woman . . . I can even make up for the part.' Her laughter tinkled and was lost on the breeze. 'I *had* seen a specialist and knew his name. That helped. Actually I was petrified that I was pregnant. All rather amusing when one looks back on it. There's a great deal to be said for the simple life. Don't look so murderous.'

'I feel murderous.'

'Trapped might be a good word, too.'

Guy turned away. He knew it was true.

'Well,' she demanded, 'what are you going to do?'

For a moment there was an ominous silence, then he said with a deadly calm that left her in no doubt of his inflexibility: 'I will arrange to pay your debts and make you a small allowance, provided you leave here by the end of the week. Stay and I shall move out of this house and if you want a penny out of me you'll have to sue me and be damned.'

Monica knew she had gone far enough.

'I'll take that,' she said condescendingly. 'Sylvia and I are going to join forces. Live in London. She made me see sense this morning when I made such a fool of myself over pleading to stay here. She knows all the answers.'

'She may do, but your allowance will continue only so long as you keep away from here—from me. That will be a condition, Monica,' he finished sternly.

'Fair enough. I've got what I came back to England for, why should I worry.' As she spoke she got up and moved to the doors leading into the house. 'Actually,' she added, 'I'm leaving tomorrow. I've already packed.'

'Then,' he said grimly, 'I shall be spared the annoyance of seeing you again. I'm going over to my father's place this evening. I shall stay the night.'

'I'd no idea you loved her so *much*,' Monica said hatefully.

'Get out,' he thundered.

She went and he stood there in what seemed a terrible silence; silence in a world of destruction, hopelessness and despair.

LORELI studied Anya with concern. She and Marcus had
been married for six weeks and now, within three days,
Anya and Graham would be walking down that same
cathedral aisle—a quiet, early morning wedding, without
fuss or fanfare. Anya's pale face and dark-rimmed eyes tore
at Loreli's heart, and she said gently: 'My dear, are you sure
about this?'

Anya rested her head back against the cushions of her
chair and surveyed Loreli with tender gratitude. A deep
friendship had sprung up between them and Loreli had
brought to Wyvern a happiness and serenity that had stilled
the disturbed, discordant atmosphere within it. Now it was
home and, in it, Anya found her only sanctuary. She had
given up her job at the hotel a week previously and all the
preparations for her marriage to Graham were complete.
Temporarily they had taken a furnished flat before making a
final decision as to where they most wanted their house
built.

'I am sure there is nothing else I can do, Loreli. At least
with any peace of mind. You know all the circumstances and
in my place wouldn't you feel the same?'

'Yes,' Loreli admitted honestly. She held her hands out to
the blazing log fire, for the November day was cold and outside snow was wrapping the countryside in a white mantle.
There was a faint pause. 'Have you heard about Guy?' she
added swiftly.

Instantly Anya was alert, every nerve tingling.

'No . . . what?'

'That he's selling the farm.'

'Oh, no!' Anya's cry was on a note of anguish. 'But it was a part of him. Green Meadows . . .' Words choked her.

'It was also a part of his misery—associated with it. I saw him the other day. I thought you'd like to know. He asked after you.'

Anya's heart dangled on a breaking thread, everything else was silent in her empty world except its heavy thudding.

'You—you told him . . .'

'He knew you were being married on Thursday.'

'Did he—did he mention *her*?'

'Only that she was in London. They never meet.' Loreli made a little sad gesture. 'It's all so futile. . . .'

'Yes—futile,' Anya agreed flatly. Her gaze rested on Loreli. 'You've been so good to me. If you knew what it has meant to come here as I have since September . . . you and Daddy . . . I think I'd have gone mad without you.' She made a wry face. 'That sounds horribly dramatic, but one can be so lost and it doesn't get any better.'

'Do you want children?' Loreli asked, her thoughts rushing ahead.

Anya winced. Graham's children, never Guy's. . . .

'Yes; but I mustn't have them for the wrong reason . . . use them to make a marriage tolerable.'

Loreli disliked Graham intensely just then. He was so happy in having achieved his own ambition, and so blind to the misery in Anya's eyes. How could a man marry, she argued, under such conditions? But almost as swiftly as the thought came to her, compassion chased after it. Love could be responsible for people behaving quite contrary to their natures—even to the best of which they were capable.

'I shall love them. So will Marcus.' There was a wistful note in Loreli's voice.

Anya glanced at the clock. In an hour Daphne and Paul would be there, joining in the quiet family dinner.

'I must go and change, I suppose,' she said wearily. 'It's

182

the keeping up; the acting and knowing that Guy's *there* . . . loving me, wanting me,' she said fiercely, 'as I love and want him.'

'That's why he's going away. . . . It could even be more dangerous once you and Graham are married.'

'Marriage seeming partly to discharge my debt?'

'You could say that. . . .'

'Two people both tied for different reasons. I wondered if she might divorce him.'

'Not a woman of her type. Marriage on her terms gives her everything she wants out of it.'

'Marriage,' murmured Anya. 'Mrs Graham Collins.' The telephone rang and without realizing it she rushed towards it, her voice breathless expectant. . . . Her heart always prayed it might be Guy, even though her mind knew it would not. Then, 'James . . . oh, how lovely to hear you.' She stopped. 'Of course we will. . . . You're special. . . . No, don't do that, I'd hate to see you hanged and it wouldn't help. . . . Yes; I've heard. New Zealand.' Her voice quivered. 'Don't talk like that; you're a link. I need you—truly.'

Loreli said as Anya replaced the receiver: 'I like James so much.'

'He's a very loyal friend. He said that Guy was going to New Zealand.' That sick panic stirred again in Anya's heart. It all seemed more than she could bear. She got up out of her chair and stood looking down at Loreli. 'You're really happy here—aren't you?'

'So happy, but it hurts me because you're not.'

'I shall be. I *must*,' Anya said fiercely. 'How long can one go on suffering? When can one forget?' She spoke half to herself and finished with Omar Khayyam's words: ' "Nor all thy Tears wash out a Word of it." '

Loreli moved from her chair and stood looking at Anya with loving gentleness. Anya bent and brushed her cheek with her lips.

'Bless you for everything—for all the joy you've brought

183

into this house, darling.' Anya gazed around her. New decorations had replaced the drab beiges and browns; a few carefully chosen pictures, artistically hung, brought life and colour to the room almost as though it had acquired some vibrant personality of its own. Even the fire itself flamed and crackled as though part of a vitality, a hope, previously missing. Marcus returned and at the sound of his key in the lock Loreli was out into the hall, her welcome a spontaneous gesture of love, the light in her eyes warming and full of promise.

Anya passed them on her way up to her room to change. She said teasingly: 'You'll loathe being alone, of course!'

Marcus chuckled. He looked so much younger that Anya felt it almost ridiculous to think in terms of his being her father. Suddenly he had become a dear friend with whom she could laugh and joke.

It struck her as she dressed and took a final look at herself in the familiar glass, that this was the last stage of her turbulent youth. . . . That room had seen her in all the depression of an earlier stagnation; it had been privy to her first thrill of love, to the wild and passionate excitement of her relationship with Guy, to the humiliation and despair of their earlier parting and, now, to the grave resignation of marriage to Graham. The face she looked at was a stranger's face, moulded into unfamiliar lines; a face which could never tell its own story . . . only the story life imposed upon it.

Downstairs she heard Daphne and Paul arriving, and the cheerful laughter and greetings that followed. Paul's divorce had gone swiftly through without complication or undue publicity. Their marriage was fixed for January 1st, the day on which the decree became Absolute. Anya's mind swung back to a conversation she'd had with Daphne immediately after their mother's death. . . . She wondered why things were so complicated for some people and so simple for others and then stopped. . . . Wasn't that because people made their own complications very often, and could she

184

say with truth that she had not done that? Guy's name was like an echo in her brain, her heart. . . . He walked beside her, his voice haunting, every word he had uttered on that last occasion repeated as her only salvation. Tears gushed to her eyes and, brushing them away, she smeared her mascara. Daphne came upon her frantically trying to repair the damage and saying, taking in the facts at a glance, but tactful enough not to betray herself:

'Oh, lord, pushed the brush in your eye? Maddening.'

Anya held a tissue against her face, swallowed hard to gain control and said, too gaily: 'Just what one loves when one's made-up. . . . How are you? Good journey?'

'Phew, good journey! Roads icy as hell—if hell is icy. But Paul's superb at getting out of skids.' She didn't look at Anya because she couldn't bear to see her dumb misery beneath that courageous brightness. 'Isn't it marvellous to be able to come home like this? To *want* to come. Loreli's fantastic, isn't she?'

Anya smiled at the adjectives. 'Fantastic,' she echoed. 'That's better. I can see you now. . . . Goodness, that's a suit.'

Daphne swung around to be admired. 'Paul chose it. Would insist on velvet. Ruby velvet. I must say I don't think I look bad in it.'

'Superb,' Anya teased.

'And you look fabulous, too,' Daphne insisted. 'That shimmery turquoisy colour is wonderful on you. . . . Graham not here yet?'

'No; he had a late appointment.'

'A crop of weddings in this family. Mine soon,' she added thrilled. 'You like Paul, don't you?'

'Very much. I like his sincerity and because he loves you.'

Daphne's eyes were stars in a cameo-like face.

'I'm a better person for that, thank God. It was the suspense that made me such a tartar. . . . It isn't exactly

185

easy to be in love with a married man. Trust can't go all the way.'

Anya was standing near the window and now the scene was like a Christmas card, as the moon threw ice blue shadows upon the whiteness of the snow and the cathedral rose, serene and permanent, to a clear sapphire sky.

'That's Graham,' she said swiftly. 'I must go.'

As she hurried past Daphne, Daphne caught her hand, squeezed it, and said huskily: 'Be happy, darling—please.' She added because of the emotion tearing at her: 'A damn silly thing to say.'

Graham held Anya in an almost stifling embrace as she reached him, looking down at her intently, kissing her and then whispering: 'You look wonderful, darling. . . . This is going to be a very happy evening . . . and when we've had dinner, I've a gift for you.'

'Graham! You've given me so much already.'

He laughed. 'Can't help myself . . . I love you.'

A pang shot through her. She held his hand tightly. 'Oh, Graham, I will do everything to make you happy. I want things to be so right between us.'

'I know you do, and they will,' he said quietly.

They went into the living-room, Daphne joined them and the evening began . . . cocktails, a perfect dinner eaten by candlelight, with Mrs Bradstock beaming like the full moon and in her element to be helping Loreli to whom she had become a devoted slave. It was as they sat over coffee, chatting idly, that the sound of a car breaking in the drive made Marcus say: 'Friends? I wonder who?'

Graham got to his feet, put down his brandy glass and said: 'Someone I took the liberty of inviting.'

Loreli flashed Marcus a startled gaze. Anya said: 'Graham!' Her tone was full of surprise.

Graham smiled. 'I'll go to the door if I may.'

The next second Anya heard Guy's voice in the hall and suppressed the startled cry that would have escaped her lips.

186

'Good lord,' Marcus said, 'isn't that Latimer?'

Guy came into the room, his expression baffled and a little wary. He looked at Marcus and then at Loreli.

'I'm sorry for this intrusion, but I was assured by Mr Collins that it was vital and urgent.'

Marcus said rather weakly: 'Oh, that's all right.'

'Of course,' agreed Loreli.

'Brandy? A drink—anything,' Marcus went on, feeling suddenly nervous—the nervousness of anxiety.

Only Anya remained silent. She met Guy's eyes, let her gaze remain in his for a second, and then looked away.

Graham began to do the talking. 'You'll probably think it odd that I want you all to hear what I've to say . . . but it's just that in the end it will be simpler. . . .' His voice dropped slightly as he went on and now he addressed Anya. 'I told you I'd a gift for you. . . that gift is your freedom . . . I can't go on with our marriage. I can't cheat you of happiness any longer.'

Marcus jerked forward in his chair.

Graham ignored the interruption and turned to Guy. 'Your wife came to see me a month ago,' he said quietly, and the air in the room seemed to chill at the sound of her name. 'I've kept quiet about it—about everything—because I was determined not to lose Anya.'

Anya gasped. 'I don't follow——'

'You will,' Graham said, and his voice sharpened the suspense. 'Mrs Latimer came to me hoping that I would repay the debt she owed you . . . and because she knew that I was the only person who *could* repay it by setting you free. . . . You see, what she told you in order to separate you from Guy was, ironically enough, *true*.'

Anya felt that every particle of her body gradually chilled; her skin seemed to lift itself from her flesh in an uncanny sensation of excitement.

'*Graham*. . . . You mean——'

As Graham stood there the scene changed, and he relived

187

those intolerable moments when Monica, ashen and pitiful, had sat opposite him, half-crazed with fear which she struggled to conceal, and said in a hollow, breathless voice: 'So you see, Mr Collins, I was so clever; I lied in every direction; about everything. . . . A year to live. . . . And she believed me. I even tried to bargain with my own life. . . . But what I didn't know, what had been kept from me by the doctors, was that every word I said was true. *True* . . . only I haven't *got* a year . . . and I've had all the treatment possible since I left Green Meadows. I've been rotten— rotten. I'm not going to be a hypocrite now. What's done, is done. But when there's nothing left but death, lies, hatred, spite have a knack of seeming very tawdry. I parted Guy and Anya . . . and even if I die at this moment, Anya won't let *you* down. That's why I've come to *you*. . . .'

Graham shivered as he met Anya's startled gaze, and he wondered if he would ever forget the look in Monica's eyes, or these weeks of tumult and conflict, when he'd done nothing that was asked of him and been determined to marry Anya at all costs.

'I mean that she *was* dying; that nothing could save her. She only learned the truth after she left Green Meadows, and when it was impossible to hide it from her any longer. Her words, her schemes——'

'Were a boomerang,' Guy said dully.

Anya cried: 'But why should she come to you?'

'The last gesture—atonement, if you like, to get me to break our engagement. She had robbed you of happiness— shattered your life and Guy's. . . . On her death she knew I should be the only stumbling block . . . and that you'd never let *me* down.'

Anya put her hands up over her face, silenced, still.

'She also told me that should the operation—the last resort—she was going to have, to any extent prolong her life, she would give Guy the evidence to divorce her. So, whichever way one looked at it, whatever happened . . .'

He stumbled over the words and Guy said quietly: 'I should be free.'

'Yes.' Graham's voice rose. 'I'd made up my mind never to tell you any of this. I was determined not to give you up, Anya, even though I promised her I would.' His face was mask-like and grim. 'These weeks have been a nightmare and suddenly I knew that I couldn't live the rest of my life cheating you, robbing you of your happiness, and I was afraid that when Guy was free—and that was inevitable anyway—you would get to hate me because, but for me, you could marry him.'

There was a heavy, dramatic silence which Guy broke.

'And you didn't know that Monica died this afternoon?'

Graham paled. 'No.'

'I had the news through the hospital. I saw her last night. She was then in a coma.' The staccato sentences hushed those listening and no words of sympathy were uttered. 'It was,' Guy added, 'merciful. I would like to add that she had already sent me the evidence necessary to get a divorce.' He looked at Anya with all the hunger that had tormented him. 'But what could I do? . . . Monica was right. . . . Only *you*' —his voice dropped on a note of deep gratitude as he went on, 'could take any steps, Graham. . . . Thank you. I can't say more.'

'I must have been mad to have remained silent at all.'

Anya said gently: 'Human. It can almost be the same thing.' She dare not look at Guy, she dare not think subjectively because of the tumult within her.

Marcus got to his feet and to the amazement of them all, said to Graham: 'I'd given you until tomorrow.'

There was a gasp from the others.

Graham turned a dull red. 'You mean——'

'I mean that Mrs Latimer wrote to me. She gave me all the facts—as a precaution. I didn't want to have to make it an issue, a threat.' He glanced down at Loreli. 'I'm sorry, darling, but a confidence is a confidence.'

189

Graham said: 'So *that's* why you've been so strange towards me. . . .'

'That's why,' said Marcus briefly.

'And now——'

'The past is—past,' said Marcus, and if I could offer you any consolation it would be to assure you that marriage without love on *both* sides can be hell, and that you have escaped it.'

Daphne, not daring to utter a word during that interminable time, gasped: 'Well! I suppose we couldn't be expected to guess all that.' She glanced at Paul. 'Or did your novelist's brain get it ages ago?'

Her words, apparently flippant, broke the unbearable tension. Paul gave her no answer.

Guy looked at Anya. 'I'd like to talk to you——' He stopped.

Anya went up to Graham. 'Thank you,' she whispered chokingly. 'Give me my last gift very soon?'

'And that?'

'To be at *your* wedding. I've been a thorn for so long—spoiled so much for you.'

Graham, just for that moment, felt a bubble of happiness light as air. The torment and the conflict were over. The jealousy and the fear were shadows that began to slither out of his life.

'I'll do my best,' he said quietly. 'Anya, be happy. I want that *reward*.'

'You shall have it,' she promised.

It was a little later that Guy and Anya went into the frosty November air.

'I'm driving you to Green Meadows,' Guy said firmly. 'I daren't begin to talk, or hardly to think until we can be quite alone.'

And at last they reached the farm which spread out against the heavens, drawing from it all the radiance of moonlight that cascaded over hills and valleys and threw

190

tapering ice blue shadows upon the old house which, in turn, traced its pattern across the snow dusted lawns that shimmered like diamond powder.

Inside Guy's study a log fire had burned to a white hot ash. No words were uttered as Guy drew her into his arms, holding her there, feeling her body trembling against his and then moving slightly so that he could look down into her eyes before kissing her.

'I love you, my darling,' he said softly. 'When all this has died down—this story of mine—will you marry me?'

She couldn't answer him, but her lips, hot and passionate beneath his own, told him all he ached to know. They found in those moments all the ecstasy, the peace and fulfilment of loving without fear, without the paralysing knowledge that in a few moments that peace would vanish and some new problem strike to tear them apart.

'But the farm,' she whispered incoherently, as they drew back from each other. 'Oh, Guy, I couldn't bear it to go.'

'Never,' he promised. 'Oh, it was true if you heard that I was selling it and going to New Zealand. . . . What did it matter? New Zealand . . . Timbuctoo . . . Without you . . .'

He didn't finish the remark for Anya pressed her cheek to his, and then said gently: 'And now even the past has lost its bitterness . . . been redeemed.'

'Yes.' The thought of Monica lay between them in understanding. 'It was an ironical ending.'

'Perhaps,' Anya murmured, 'I was meant to believe what was, after all, the truth . . . perhaps in a case like that, instinct has validity. . . . If I'd refused to believe her could we know quite the happiness of these moments?'

'No,' he agreed. 'Oh, my dearest, the torment of thinking of your marriage; the knowledge that I should, in any case, be free . . . It was utter hell because I couldn't do anything about it. I could only have made you more miserable.'

Her sigh was full of an ecstatic content that seemed to flow over her body like a tide. She pressed her face close to his shoulder and clung to him, feeling his arms about her—a protection, a sanctuary.

'It isn't possible,' she whispered, 'that anyone's life can change so miraculously in a matter of hours.

'There was just something in Graham's voice when he asked me over to Wyvern that gave me hope,' Guy admitted. 'Heaven knows I'm sorry for him. I hope life won't be so grim for him as it has been for me without you.'

'I wonder why,' Anya said, 'it takes less courage to hurt oneself than to hurt another person?... Oh, Guy, I love you so much—so much.'

Their lips met and all the peace of that still night was the promise of their future and of their happiness.